Advance Praise

"Monica Bhide's short story collection isn't impressive because it's a first-timer's effort—it's impressive, period. The stories, each filled with strong, feisty characters and exquisite details of people, places, and things, will keep you riveted. There are plenty of Indian Americans writing novels these days, but far too few writing short stories and even fewer writing stories of this caliber."

> — Sree Sreenivasan, co-founder of the South Asian Journalists Association and Chief Digital Officer at The Metropolitan Museum of Art

"This book and its characters will haunt you long after you finish reading it."

> — Kathleen Flinn, author of the New York Times bestseller *The Sharper Your Knife, the Less You Cry*

"Monica Bhide's shimmering short stories travel from Maryland to Mumbai and back again, effortlessly introducing us to soldiers and shape-shifters, hijras and housewives. With insightful grace, she illuminates the ordinary miracles and tragedies of suburban American life, intertwined with an India equally intimate and spectacular. Full of rich, delicate details

and searing character portraits, these remarkable stories remind us of the demons we carry inside us on all of our journeys."

— Annia Ciezadlo, author of *Day of Honey: A Memoir of Food, Love, and War*

"Monica Bhide's excellent collection will transport you to unexpected places, moving you between America and India, hospitals, college campuses, ancient temples, a devastated train station. You will be entranced by the wide spectrum of characters she has created—a newlywed doctor learning to love his wife, a cancer survivor hoping for a second chance, a dying old man filled with hate, a transsexual who adopts a young orphan. Filled with surprises and heart, this book will pull you in and not let you go."

— Chitra Divakaruni, author of *Oleander Girl* and *Mistress of Spices*

"Monica Bhide's wonderful, internationally-flavored collection is full of spice and life. The beguiling voice of a true storyteller will lure you out of your self into her intriguing, fictional world. Enjoy!"

— Diana Abu-Jaber, author of *Crescent* and *Bird of Paradise*

"For those of us who know Monica's superb food writing, this book will not surprise you. It's written with the same clarity, warmth, and attention to detail as you might expect from her. But what you may not expect is to see the emergence of a fiction writer to be reckoned with—these stories have heart and characters that will stay with you long after you close the book."

— Mollie Cox Bryan, author of the Agatha-Award nominated *Scrapbook of Secrets: A Cumberland Creek Mystery*

Monica Bhide's riveting collection of short stories brings out the complex flavors of modern day families across the globe. Filled throughout with movement and truly international in its reach, this book is certain to keep you captivated.

— Sweta Srivastava Vikram, Amazon bestseller and award-winning author.

"Monica Bhide's debut short story collection takes us on a journey of an India that few of us know. In wise, compassionate prose, she tells us stories of love, longing and redemption, weaving in the India of temples, rituals and arranged marriages with a much darker side. And memories and fantasies of the homeland continue to resonate in her tales of contemporary Indian American life. Novelistic in scope, this book effortlessly bridges both worlds and signals the emergence of a strong new voice in fiction."

— A.X. Ahmad, author of *The Caretaker* and *The Last Taxi Ride*

"Indian-American short fiction that will tear your heart apart and sew it back together with thin threads of hope. A must-read for those who like their stories raw and real. THE DEVIL IN US, will put the devil in you, because you won't be able to put this down!"

— Jessica Bell, Publishing Editor of *Vine Leaves Literary Journal*

"Monica Bhide beguiling writing takes us into the rich tapestry within private, intimate worlds that we don't want to leave."

— Shoba Narayan, James Beard award-winning author of the memoirs, *Monsoon Diary* and *Return to India*.

The Devil in Us

Stories of Love, Life, and Redemption

Monica Bhide

Outside my window there is a tree
There is a bird
There is light
A blue sky
Each day it promises a new beginning
I draw the curtains.
The light hurts my eyes.

—Monica Bhide

True purity is often tarnished.

—Tao

CONTENTS

The Devil in Us 1

The Soul Catcher 9

Karma and the Art of Redemption 23

Longings 29

A Beautiful Boy..71

Home Alone 93

Best Friends 119

True Love 145

The Prize of War...159

The Vermillion Promise...177

The Run 187

Doubts..217

Dear John 227

Glossary 233

Acknowledgements 235

About the Author..237

The Devil in Us

Dr. Anand, with his freshly trimmed beard and his freshly washed pants and white shirt, and his new wife, Sonia, sporting a tight, red beaded *salwaar kameez*, were on his new bike as they headed to her new job. Sonia fidgeted and tried to cover her head with her red and golden *dupatta* to save her hair from the Mumbai humidity and dust.

"This is a blessing from Lord Krishna," Sonia said before they left their newly rented room. A small space, but as she pointed out to him, "It is clean and has running water." It had a bed and a small area to serve as a kitchen, and they shared a bathroom with the rest of the floor. She had set it up so that the room was divided into four clear spaces: a place to sleep, a place for her small temple, a place where they liked to play cards, and a small spot for her Singer, a machine that had helped her sew the clothes she was wearing today for her first day at her new job.

"Yes, it is," he nodded, touching the gleaming gold pendant around his neck. The word *OM* was with him constantly thanks to the pendant his wife's father had given him at their wedding three weeks ago.

Today their new life was to truly start, a gift from Krishna indeed.

He worked at a small government clinic about ten kilometers from their newly rented room and she was going to work at the cafeteria of a call center just outside Mumbai. She needed to take the train to work. "Let's have some breakfast at the train station today, a treat to start a new life?" he had offered.

They were still formal with each other. She knew very little about him, but her father had convinced her that Anand was the right choice.

She had not let him touch her yet. "How do people in arranged marriages sleep with their partners?" she had asked her friend. "Sex and love have nothing to do with each other," the wise seventeen-year-old had responded. Still, Sonia could not let a man she did not know come near her. Dr. Anand did not seem to mind … yet. She would often observe him as he slept. His defiant chin seemed gentle when he slept, his normally perfect hair fell in unruly curls over his face. He always rested his right hand on his forehead as he slept and when he was in a real, deep sleep, he snored louder than the train that seemingly ran all day behind their building.

She wondered if she could have done better. "He is so boring," she told her sister. "He seems okay. Maybe this doctor thing will make him some money and you will get a television, the first one in the family," her sister had said. He was a sissy, a coward, Sonia thought; he had not even tried to touch her. She had taken that as a clue and established herself as the stronger one in the house.

"Anand, we will live here by my rules now. This is my house."

He just smiled. A sissy, she told her sister repeatedly, he is a sissy. Yes, her sister had replied, but hopefully a rich sissy soon. "Maybe he will leave the government clinic and start his own practice and then, then, you will have a fridge to go with the TV he will get you."

"Here we are," Anand said as he stopped the gleaming bike near his favorite breakfast cart outside the main train station. He had scrubbed the bike hard, making sure it shined. "It should look like it belongs to a doctor, not a pharmacy worker," Sonia joked as she helped him clean it, all the time singing tunelessly and avoiding eye contact with him.

He could not believe his luck. How had this beautiful creation ever agreed to marry a simpleton like him? He loved her smell—he had not yet found the nerve to ask her what soap she used, but she smelled of jasmine constantly. He watched as she dried her hair and made him tea in the mornings, watched the way her long wet hair covered her ample bosom, the way her hands moved sensually as she picked out the cups and poured the amber liquid, the way in which she cupped her hands around the teacup and blew gently into the tea to cool it down before it touched her luscious lips. Yes, Krishna be thanked, she was perfect. He could not wait to touch her but wanted it to be by choice, not by force. His buddies shared what they thought were funny wedding night stories, "I could not find where to put it in," said one, and another one said his wife screamed all night. Dr. Anand was horrified. Where were their manners? But, he consoled himself, these now married friends were in their late twenties and still virgins. All they wanted to do was have sex as soon as possible after the ceremony so desperation was bound to come along and take over any sense of romance or even common sense. He could wait.

At night when Sonia slept, he would take out his notebook, the one he kept hidden inside the small cupboard in the kitchen. He wrote poetry about her eyes, her hair, her lips. And then he drew her picture. Again and again and again.

The morning rush was evident everywhere as the train station, like an overstuffed *samosa*, tried to contain everyone. People were rushing to or from work, walking purposefully and filling every inch of the earth around them.

Just as they were about to order their tea, there was a loud sound.

A sound unlike Dr. Anand or Sonia had ever heard filled the air.

It sounded like a blast, like an earthquake, like the earth splitting open, the ground giving way, bombs going off.

He left the bike in front of the tea stall and rushed into the station toward the noise, leaving a stunned Sonia behind screaming, "Don't go, Anand, don't leave me, where are you going? Come back! What is going on? Hey *Bhagwan*, help us!"

It took Dr. Anand only a second to realize what had happened. One of the local trains had rammed into another at full speed. Both seemed to have been ripped apart at the seams, green doors and broken windows everywhere. Metal and bodies were intertwined. People were running in every direction. The shrill sounds of death screams filled the air.

Blood and body parts cluttered the platform. Screams about terror, bombs, fire, blood, emanated from everywhere.

Dr. Anand ran toward the trains.

Sonia, scared of waiting alone, followed him, running breathlessly, unsure of what to do. A man rushed past her into the road holding the side of his head which was bleeding profusely, a section of his skull on display to the world. A woman in a gray sari ran by screaming, her hair on fire, her face barely visible. Someone pushed her to the ground, others began to throw the water from their bottles on her, still others screamed for shawls or blankets to put the fire out. The fire department's screeching horn added to the noise. Hundreds and thousands of people were running toward the trains. Sonia thought, *should they not be running away?* She stopped short of entering the station. It was the most chilling yet strangely amazing sight she had ever seen.

Strangers lifted strangers out of the rubble. Cops in khaki-colored uniforms appeared and began to try to organize the crowds. Out on the road, people stopped their cars, mopeds, cycles, buses, everything, and offered to drive strangers to the hospital. *"Lauker, lauker, pani, pani!"* (Fast, fast, water, water!) In so many languages, so many tongues screaming the same thing. Water, we need water.

Sonia ran into the station to look for Anand.

She saw a young man lying on the side of a train track, his arms gone, blood pooling everywhere. She rushed to help him. Beside him were a pair of a baby's booties, no baby, but the booties still had feet in them. She held back her vomit, trying to cover her nose and mouth with her red and golden dupatta.

She wanted to put her arms around his waist and drag him toward the road, but couldn't, she simply froze as she stared down at the life flowing away from his body and his pleading eyes begging her for help. Suddenly, several people appeared out of nowhere, pulling him, placing him on a large piece of wood, rushing him to an already overcrowded ambulance.

A horrible stench filled the air. Later, Anand would tell her it was the smell of burning human and animal flesh. Dogs were lying crushed under the weight of the torn trains and their decapitated passengers.

She turned and saw Dr. Anand, his fresh white shirt covered in blood and soot, kneeling on the ground. He was using bits of cloth to bandage someone's arm. Mobile phones of the dead were ringing, loudly—popular tunes, religious songs, lullabies that now sounded harsh, gruesome. Anand and Sonia helped as they could. They moved back as more ambulances arrived and the cops began to load people in by the dozen.

Dr. Anand walked toward the end of the platform. Some people had been thrown twenty feet away from the train. The platform was filled with ghoulish bloody footprints, and people ran over the pouring streams of human blood, excrement, and body parts.

An old man dressed in white pants and a green shirt was lying on his back, his face bloody and his arm dangling lifelessly from his thin frame. Dr. Anand bent down to help. The man, still conscious, pulled away from Anand's touch and pointed to the gold pendant shining brightly around Anand's neck. "You are Hindu! *Your* people did this. But they will blame us." The man's harsh words startled Dr. Anand. "Your people will say the Muslims did this. Now you wish to help me? Go away." Dr. Anand regained his composure and calmly responded, "I am a doctor. Now give me your arm and let me stop the bleeding or you are going to die here, right now. This was a train accident, not a terrorist attack. Look, look there … the trains rammed into each other."

The man pulled away and tried to scream, "Don't you dare touch me."

Dr. Anand got up and shook his head. He looked around the station; the morning sun was hotter and the air was now filled with the nauseating stench of death. He looked around to see if there was someone else he could help. Suddenly he felt a gentle tap on his shoulder. He turned around to find Sonia looking frightened, with tears pouring down her cheeks.

"Come on, let's go find the bike," Dr. Anand said finally. "Stupid fucks. Now there will be more deaths, more finger-pointing, and now there will be goddamn bombs. This, Sonia, this is what stupid people do to each other. Look." They turned to watch the man who had pulled away from Dr. Anand struggle to catch his breath. The man looked up at them and then spit in Dr. Anand's direction.

Dr. Anand and Sonia turned and walked toward the exit of the train station.

Burning flesh, scorching hair, screaming babies. Sonia found a corner and began to throw up. Again and again. A street vendor came up and gave her a coconut filled with cool coconut water. *"Piyo, piyo,"* he urged her to drink. She reached in her purse for money. "No, no," he said, and walked away.

"This is so horrible. I cannot believe it, Anand. You … you have … I … you … I, you have such strength. "

They walked to the bike, hand in hand. "Accidents happen. Let us thank Krishna that we were here in time to help. Now, let's go back home," he whispered.

Back in the security of their room, he went to his cupboard and fished under a pile of his neatly folded clothes. He pulled out a bottle of rum and within an hour downed the entire hot, burning, "soother" as he called it. He began to talk, nonstop. At first his painful words made a lot of sense and then no sense as he got totally drunk. "People are so horrible sometimes. What was the point of this? Can you tell me? Can anyone tell me? We make advances in medicine, we become doctors so we can save people but now, now people won't let me save them. I don't understand. And that man, telling me not to touch him. Those are the people who cause all these problems. They are responsible. I guess we are all responsible … I guess … God help us all."

She walked over and sat down next to him on the bed. Then she placed her head on his shoulder and held his hand.

Her father was right. She had married the right man.

The Soul Catcher

The amber flame is tiny and potent. The candle burns slowly, radiating sweet scents of musk and frangipani. The wafting floral scents give life. But more importantly and without any remorse, they also take it away.

The flame burns steadily this evening, it barely flickers. It knows, perhaps, someone is going to die tonight.

Yamini gracefully places the candle on a small golden candleholder. She sets it down on the tiny brown coffee table alongside fresh white roses in a crystal vase, a well-worn book about the Vietnam War, and a jar filled with Christmas cookies. She has been here before and knows the room well. It is filled with photos of his life. A few show him and his buddies on their ship; there are two with his sons, one with his wife, Janet, taken on their wedding day sixty years ago (as she told Yamini).

"It is so nice for a young woman like you to volunteer here. Now tell me, what does your name mean? It is so unusual," Janet had said to her earlier that week.

Yamini smiled. It was a question she was often asked. "My mother was living in India when I was born. It was a moonless night and dark outside, so she named me Yamini—it means 'night.' She told me that it isn't always the light that brings good things, sometimes the darkness can bring better things in life."

In just a few minutes of conversation, Yamini heard what she needed: "We decided to bring Tim here because it is time for us to let him go. He is my high school sweetheart, you know? I sense in my heart he is ready to leave now. I just need to make him as comfortable as I can," Janet said as she gazed lovingly at her dying husband.

Now the old man on the bed stirs and calls for his wife. "Janet, is that you? Janet?" The room is dim but for the orangey glow of the black candle. Yamini moves slowly toward the old man, dragging her feet, with painful steps.

"I can do this," she mutters and pulls herself to the bed using her hands. Her strength is draining, there is little time left.

The sweet scent from the candle finds its way into every crevice. The scents have found their destination.

Yamini is grateful the bed is low. She sits beside Tim and holds his cold, wrinkled hand, and he calls for his wife again.

"Tim, thank you for calling me. I am Yamini. You appeared in my dream and asked for relief. I am here now, and I promise, you will not be in pain anymore," she says, placing her carefully manicured hand over his forehead.

He grips her other hand even tighter and opens his eyes. "You have come," he mumbles. "Say goodbye to Janet for me … I love her so much."

She tries to smile at him but the pain sears through her chest and her legs and she flinches.

"When the visions come, you have to act on them, otherwise you will die a slow and painful death. You will spread light through your darkness. You are the soul catcher," a fortuneteller in New Delhi had told her when she was five. And now, here she is, the soul catcher, a hundred years later. She closes her eyes and begins to chant a soft verse of love and living forever, of dying and being reborn, of giving and gratitude.

From the center of his forehead, a cool sensation moves up her hand and into her heart.

She opens her eyes and he closes his forever.

"Thank you for your help," she whispers and kisses his forehead.

The flame dies. The scent is gone. The only smell that lingers is the lemony cleaning liquid used to mop the floors earlier that morning. Everything is the same and yet, everything is now different.

Yamini picks up the candle and its holder and places them in her tiny leather pouch.

"Please, come in, now we cannot delay," Yamini calls out and a young man, Roger, opens the door and rushes in with a wheelchair. The glow from the light in the corridor spills onto the wooden floor of the room.

Roger grimaces when he sees the silhouette of the man on the bed. It is too dark to see anything clearly.

"Is, is that him?"

"Now, now, we need to go, we don't have time," she says and bends over as the pain worsens.

"Are you okay, Yamini?" He touches her shoulder.

Roger struggles to get her tiny frame into the wheelchair. She looks frail, almost waif-like but he cannot seem to lift her. He pulls her arms with all his might and is finally able to get her off the bed.

I need to move. She said this would happen, it is okay, this is all going to be okay, he mutters to himself as he uses his hand to wipe away the droplets of sweat from his forehead.

She had warned him that they would have a few minutes before the hospice staff discovered the body. She knew their routine. They would be in at nine to check on Mr. Tim Wilson.

He peeks out the door. The staff is busy watching TV and bantering about Christmas reindeer and how Rudolph is actually a female reindeer since a male reindeer would lose his way.

The hospital where Roger's wife is dying is about twenty minutes away. He pushes the wheelchair as fast as he can, and reaches the end of the corridor when he hears the commotion behind him. He stops and turns to see what they are doing.

"Poor Mr. Wilson. And on Christmas Eve," says the woman dressed in a loud holiday sweater. She doesn't seem surprised; this is after all, a place where people come to die.

"I think we should wait to call Janet. She just left to be with her grandson, barely twenty minutes ago," says the tall blond woman.

They both look at each other and then the tall one says, "Okay, I will go and call her now and you call Fred at the funeral home."

Roger rushes towards the exit of the building. He has heard enough.

Lord, please forgive me, please forgive me, his muttering gets louder the faster he pushes.

"Sir, sir, you okay? She seems like she sick. You need help? You want me to call an ambulance?" The security guard at the exit catches Roger by surprise.

This is no ordinary hospice, it is where the rich come to die. The reception area has shiny floors, a chandelier dripping with crystals, sofas with silk cushions and red poinsettias all around. And they have a full-time guard. With a gun.

Roger stares at the guard standing between him and the exit to the parking lot. There is no other way out. On the left is a mammoth, well-decorated Christmas tree with wrapped boxes under it and on the right is the guard's table.

"Sir, I am asking you again, you need help? She okay?"

"Yes, she is fine. She, she is ill so she sleeps sometimes," Roger lies as he begins to sweat more profusely.

"Are you sure? Man, she looked fine when ya'll came in, she wasn't in no chair then." The guard is now staring at the well-coiffed young woman slumped in the chair. Her striking pink blouse is tight, revealing a perfectly shaped bosom, and her jeans are tucked into high-heeled boots.

"I know I've seen her here before, same thing each time, she comes in looking fine, and then some dude is always wheeling her out. What's up with that?"

"Nothing, I don't know what you are talking about. We have never been here before."

"Listen, man, whatever is going on, you need to tell me before I ..." The guard instinctively moves his hands toward his pistol.

Roger squirms in his jeans and sweater. "I, I, she is my sister and we just visited my uncle. He is ill and she gets very upset when she sees him. She will be fine. That is it, man. We just came to see him for Christmas ..."

The guard eyes them skeptically. "I know I have seen her before. I don't know about you, but I have seen her here before. Sir, I think you better wait here, I am going to call my supervisor."

Yamini stirs and moves her hand a touch. Suddenly, the guard's attention is diverted. There is a loud noise from the back of the building. "Sweet Jesus, that sounds like a gunshot, wait here, I will be right back." The guard runs toward the inside of the building.

"Now, run," whispers Yamini, "Run, Roger, run."

Roger breaks into a run, pushing as hard as he can, the weight of the chair getting heavier and heavier. The night is dark, no moon, and it seems no stars.

He struggles to get her in the car, pulling her by her arms and then finally lifting her as he would a small child.

"Leave the wheelchair here, I will come back for it later," she says.

Roger moves the wheelchair to the side of the parking lot.

"You, I told you to wait, hold on there," calls the security guard, but Roger runs back to the car.

His driving could have broken records for speed.

Roger keeps asking, "Yamini, are you all right? God, what have we done! You, we, you killed a man … what did you do? I don't know how this will help Mary …"

"It is all to save your wife. Now hurry … I don't have much time. I cannot carry him for too long," she says and closes her eyes.

Roger looks at her, puzzled, then presses down on the accelerator.

Visiting hours are over at the hospital for the regular visitors but the ICU allows family to come in anytime.

He places Yamini in a wheelchair that he finds at the entrance to the hospital.

"I know it is just supposed to be me but today, just once, please, just once, it is Christmas Eve and this may be the last time we are together. My sister here is very ill too and this may be our last …." His pleading works with the night staff.

Mary lies on her hospital bed, but it is hard to tell there is a person buried under all those tubes.

"Her body is shutting down, one organ at a time," her doctor had told him two days ago.

Each time he came in to see her, the tubes going into her body seemed to multiply.

It was during his last visit, he was sitting in the cafeteria sipping coffee and staring at the paper in his hand. Her doctor had given him a piece of paper and said, "I think you should take a look at this." A "DO NOT RESUSCITATE" order.

"You can save her, you know. You don't need to sign that paper," a young woman, a complete stranger, said as she sat across from him at the table.

"I am sorry, do I know you?" Roger asked.

The woman smiled. "No, of course you don't. I know your wife is dying and I know how to save her. I can help."

"I am sorry, I am not interested in whatever it is you are selling," Roger stood up to leave. "My wife is dying and you are trying to scam me? Really? This just sucks."

"Mr. Roger. Please stop. I am not trying to sell you anything. If you walk away, you will lose your only chance to save Mary. I know her kidneys have shut down, I know her lungs are filled with water, I know her liver is failing. I know she hasn't opened her eyes or moved or said a word in months and they don't even know why she is dying. I know it all. I can help."

"How the hell do you know our names? Who gave you her medical information? I should report you. Who the hell do you think you are?" Roger began to scream as tears ran down his cheeks. "What kind of a horrible woman are you? My wife is dying and you are trying to use it to sell me an impossible dream? The doctors have suggested that I take her off life support. It is over, do you hear me, over!"

"Okay, fine, let's have it your way. If it is over then how does it hurt you to give me a chance to help her? I am not asking for anything in return. Just that you trust me. I can help you."

Roger stared long and hard at the woman. Her dark hair was thick and wavy, her face glowed, and she had some serious curves. She could have been a model if it weren't for the fact that she could barely reach over the table. Dressed in a tailored suit and carrying a Coach bag, she didn't appear to be in need of money.

He sat back down. "What can you do to help her? I will give you all that I have if you save her. I have a small house and some cash. I can give you everything. I ... I mean ... I cannot believe I am asking you this ... can you really save her?"

"I can. Now listen to me. My name is Yamini."

And now, here they were, at Mary's door.

The night nurse wasn't pleased. "Mr. Roger, Mary is not doing well, as you know, and I cannot let anyone who is ill visit her. She is critical, as you know."

"Please, just this once, we will never be able to say goodbye, I feel like her time has come," he said and began to cry. Yamini, still in the wheelchair, opens her eyes, "Please let me see her. I love her so. I just want to say goodbye."

The nurse relents. It is Christmas Eve and she would rather be home with her loved ones.

"I am so sorry. I wish things were better," the nurse said and leaves Roger and Yamini in the room and closes the door.

Yamini manages to lift herself off the wheelchair and begins to drag her feet towards the room.

The whizzing machines, the beeping sounds filling the room make Roger cry even more. Mary should be surrounded by sounds of laughter, of crying babies, of singing birds, not this.

Yamini moves to Mary's bedside and turned to Roger. "Please give me a minute."

Reluctantly, Roger turns to go out. He stops and turns back to Yamini. "Please, please help her. She is my whole life."

Yamini smiles. She turns back to Mary and waits for the sound of the closing door.

This time the candle flame burns bright, strong. A regular candle would set off the alarm as fire is not allowed inside an ICU. A sweet scent fills the room and mingles with the existing scent of bleach and decaying flesh.

Yamini grips Mary's hand with one hand and places her other hand on Mary's forehead. The sensation passes from her hand to Mary's body and her hand now feels warm.

Yamini sings her song again; this time with a smile. She knows her own nightmares will go away for now. While it is good that Mary will live, Yamini is delighted as she feels the pain leave her body. Her legs feel strong again, her hands are no longer quivering, she straightens her back and raises her hands toward the sky. "Mercy, my Lord, thank you for your mercy. I am grateful to you, my Lord, I am so grateful."

Yamini blows out the candle and places it in her pouch and then she walks out the door to Roger.

"By tomorrow morning, she will be fine. Oh, and you will name your first born for me. That is my only request!"

Roger stares at her. She is walking, more like gliding, and a few minutes ago she was dragging her legs as though they were anchored to the floor and she had to pull them out each step of the way. There is a glow on her face and she now looks peaceful, and oddly enough, younger than before. He shakes his head. Perhaps his tired mind is playing tricks on him. And this woman now seems certifiably crazy. Here Mary is dying and this woman is talking about babies.

He leaves her there and rushes to be with Mary.

"I hope I haven't done something stupid," he mutters as he walks in. Mary looks exactly the same as she did moments ago and as she has for the past six months. He moves close to her bed, holds her hand, and begins to weep. "I am so sorry Mary. I thought, I really thought, she could do something. I don't know what I was thinking. Mary, I love you. What am I going to do without you?"

Inside the room, the noises from the machines seem louder than ever. Roger clutches at Mary's hand. "Don't go, please don't go. What will I do without you?"

He moves her hand to his lips.

All of a sudden, the machines start beeping. A loud alarm goes off and the night nurse comes rushing in.

"Oh, no, no no no, Mary, don't leave me, Mary ..."

He is weeping and trembling so hard that he fails to notice that Mary has opened her eyes and is looking at him.

Several nurses and an older man, the doctor on duty, all rush in and begin to remove her breathing tube. "She is choking," someone yells. And then suddenly, they are all quiet.

Roger, who has been pushed behind the nurses, falls to the ground.

"Mary, no, no, Mary, you cannot die. Mary ...."

The stunned night nurse walks over to Roger and places her hands on his shoulders.

"Your Christmas wish seems to have been granted. She is breathing on her own and look at the machines. All her vitals are normal. I, I don't know what is going on. She is breathing on her own."

Yamini returns to the hospice. The guard is standing outside the main door, smoking.

"Hi there, I was here earlier. Sorry we could not wait then."

Even as he towers over her, he is clearly startled when he sees her tiny form.

"Look at you, ain't nothing wrong with you. You, I knew it. Look at you now. You are walking, talking, and all of it. I thought you had trouble walking," he stubs out his cigarette. "I need to call my boss."

"Wait, wait, I can explain, just give me a second to explain …?" She smiles at him with her larger-than-life smile, her glow brighter now, her black eyes glittering.

"You got thirty seconds and don't try anything smart. I have a gun and I know how to use it."

"No, I won't. I am a believer in peace and am a messenger of God."

The guard nods uncomfortably; she is beginning to weird him out.

"At least can we go inside, it is freezing out here and I do not have my jacket on," she says walking toward the entrance of the building.

He walks in behind her, unsure at first, but then he reaches for his pistol to make sure it is there.

"Can we sit at your desk there? I can explain everything. Please. I have done nothing wrong. Just give me a chance to explain."

He nods and sits down at his desk. She sits across from him.

"Make it quick, I don't have all night, come on. What is the deal with the wheelchair and am I right … oh, and you know, the last time you left, someone died. I thought nothing of it. Happened again tonight, lady. You want to explain that?"

Yamini sits quietly and then scrunches her face. "This place stinks of cigarettes. Mind if I light a small candle here and then we can talk?"

"What the hell? You want to light a fucking candle? This chat is over!"

"Please, it is just to help clear this air. I hate the smell of cigarettes."

He looks at the strange woman sitting in front of him. She is beautiful.

"Fine, light your damn candle and then spill it, lady, or I am calling the boss."

Yamini places the black candle on the gold plate and lights it.

"Smoking kills, you know," she says as the flame comes alive.

Karma and the Art of Redemption

I hate God.

I hate my life.

I hate my world.

My mother tells me my fate is determined by karma. I must have been bad in my previous life so bad things are happening to me.

Karma? What about this life? I have never harmed anyone before.

This is fucking karma?

Where does your spirit go when you die? My mother thinks we come back.

Come back!

Why in hell would anyone want to come back?

I guess it doesn't matter really.

I am going to find out soon enough.

The chilly winds feel razor-sharp on my skin.

My tears are gone. Long gone.

I am here now to make things right.

That is all that matters.

Everything is fading into the distance.

I failed. I killed my child. I failed.

I reach out to hold onto the railing of the bridge to steady myself.

All the despair, the desperateness of the past two days is gone.

My friends used to tell me that love and hate are the strongest emotions. They are wrong. There is only one strong emotion: hopelessness.

Hopelessness seeps in and creeps into your soul, until there is nowhere to hide, nowhere to run, nowhere to go.

The icy wind numbs my nose, burns my eyes, and freezes my ears; nature knows a traitor when it sees one and offers me a fitting welcome.

Maybe if I am lucky, I will die right here, right now, of hypothermia. But that would be too kind; no mercy killing for me.

I used to love this bridge.

My sister and I often joked that Key Bridge held the keys to all possibilities. Dad would pile us into the car on Saturday mornings and, despite protests from my mother, drive us into Georgetown. The bridge crossed a chasm from an area of yuppie nobodies into a paradise of the rich and famous.

He regaled us with stories of his alma mater Georgetown University: how he graduated in the same class as the amazing Dr. Sorensen, who discovered something my young mind never comprehended, and did we know that several presidents graduated from Georgetown, including the current one?

Dad is gone. Long gone. I am glad he isn't here to see how his daughter killed his grandchild.

Meeta, my sister, my younger sister who I have loved, has not bothered to call me. She blames me for Payal's death. She is right. I am responsible.

I am. I am a killer.

As a child, I wanted to be here forever on this magical bridge that took me to Georgetown.

Everybody's forever is different.

If not in life, I will be here forever in death.

I can hear the Potomac rushing below.

I look down through the haze of my tears. I thought I had no more tears left. The river is usually peaceful. Today it is gushing, rushing, alive. It is offering me my forever.

Now I wonder which boulder I will hit first when I jump.

Will death be instant?

Or will it be a slow drowning death as the water seeps into my lungs and I struggle to breathe? Will my body smell after I die? Will it swell? Perhaps it will rot beyond belief and save Nikhil the embarrassment and inconvenience of identifying me.

Nikhil, the love of my life.

Nikhil, my high school sweetheart.

Nikhil, who forgave me for what I did.

Nikhil, who should have thrown me off the deck as well, but instead hugged and cried with me.

What karma is he being punished for?

I left him sleeping in the bed this morning. He says he is coping. All the sleeping pills he takes to just help him close his eyes tell another story.

I wanted to leave him a note. But then did not. What could I have said?

Sorry? Forgive me?

I brace myself against the tall green rails. They are really high; I had not noticed that before. I will have to climb up to jump.

The fall sky becomes quiet. The wind dies down.

I hesitate. I can't bring myself to jump. I hate myself.

I am a good coward. I do it well. Perhaps it is the only thing in my life that I do well.

My hesitation bothers me.

My child, my beautiful baby girl, Payal.

Will her soul ever forgive me?

I replay the scene in my mind again and again and again. We were playing on the deck for what seemed like hours. I picked her up and threw her in the air. She laughed and giggled. I did it again and again. And then, again, and I lost my balance. She screamed as she fell head first on the concrete several feet below the deck. And she was gone.

My tiny baby was no more because of my carelessness. My stupidity. My idiocy.

I begin to breathe steadily.

I close my eyes, I am ready to go: It's now or never.

I hear a voice in my head. What about Simar?

Simar. What will happen to him?

His birth was the happiest day of my life.

His curly hair, his big brown eyes, his tinkling giggles, his love of toy cars.

It is his third birthday. Tomorrow. Tomorrow is his third birthday.

How could I have forgotten that?

I have killed one child. And now, my gift to my other one: his father telling him on his third birthday that his mother is dead.

I don't know what to do.

I should be dead. My baby should be alive.

And Simar. What about Simar?

At three, what has he done to have a dead sister? And a soon-to-be dead mother? What karma is he being punished for?

The phone in my pocket rings.

It is now or never.

I pull myself up.

The phone keeps ringing.

I take it out and look at it.

"HOME" is calling. There is a picture on the screen of me, Payal, Simar, and Nikhil.

Home calling.

I sit down on the side of the bridge.

Home is still calling.

It starts to rain.

Perhaps my child forgives me as the heaven sheds its tears to wash my evil sin. Perhaps.

I turn around and walk back to what is left of my life.

Longings

Here was the new modern India Leena had seen so many times on satellite TV at her home in Washington, DC. Each time the Indian MTV generation showed up on the screen, Leena's *dadi*, her father's mom, rolled her eyes. "See these girls, do they have no shame? They wear no clothes! I just don't understand how their parents allow them to dress like this. Even girls in America do not dress like this!" Once the rant started, Dadi would get a glint in her eyes and her voice would get louder. "*Beta*, our generation, now we knew how to dress to, you know, to be attractive for the men. Our flowing silk *dupattas* in all their colors, our graceful saris ... Poets have written beautiful verses on our clothes. Now look, look at this girl, look at that, that bandage she is wearing across her chest ... what can a poet say about that?? Hey, *Bhagwan!*"

And here Leena was, live and in person in India—a newer, younger, hipper India, seemingly so comfortable in its new skin. Leena stood in the middle of Mumbai's new airport, mesmerized at the larger-than-life images of Bollywood heroes staring down at her. The peacock motif seemed to be everywhere. "You know, the new airport is designed by the guys who designed the Burj Khalifa in Dubai," her sister,

Tania, had told her while also doing some serious begging. "You are just going for a break, right? And you don't know anyone there. I could come with you and we could backpack through the back alleys of India ... Let me come with you? Please? It will be fun!" Tania could be very persuasive. But Dadi had put her foot down. "Tania, what if you go and I fall down the stairs? I will be like that commercial you make fun of: *I have fallen and I cannot get up!* She needs a break. Let her go alone to Mumbai."

Now at Mumbai airport, Leena noticed each ear had a cell phone. Even the lanky, greasy-haired porter helping her with her bags had a cell phone in his hand. "Taxi?" he had asked and she had nodded.

Everyone everywhere looked purposeful, so connected to the rest of the Universe. Everyone had someone to talk to, someone to connect with. AT&T's "reach out and touch someone" plan surely must have originated here, she thought. A city struggling for a new identity, with a colorful past that competed with an even more colorful future, for a present that did not know which way to go and so turned toward a tomorrow that promised it all.

She felt out of place, suddenly even more conscious of her hair that had barely grown back in. She tried to straighten out her faded jeans and old t-shirt in a feeble attempt to feel presentable. Dressing up had never been one of her passions; that honor went to her younger sister, Tania. Perfect all the time. Even when she got out of bed in the mornings, she looked flawlessly groomed. Leena remembered a summer they spent in Myrtle Beach. It was 110 degrees. No one ventured outside; instead they all decided to go to the indoor pool in the hotel. Tania went for a walk—fully clothed, of course, and fully made up. She returned an hour later with a generously built young man on her arm, and glowing through the sweat beads on her forehead. Leena, in a tattered old swimsuit, was sweating puddles. *Tania would fit right in here in Mumbai. Maybe I should have let her come*, Leena thought.

Her beeping cell phone interrupted her thoughts.

"Beta, there? Suhani coming to pick you up. You know, Suhani, your relative." Dadi's texting was short and to the point as she worried about how much money each word cost her.

"Walking to parking lot, Dadi. Girls here do have clothes on," Leena texted back. Of course, she had no idea what Suhani looked like but asking Dadi that would be like asking someone to describe the Universe in two sentences or less.

"Love you, Beta. God bless you. And don't lie."

Leena just kept in step behind the porter who whizzed passed throngs of people with trolleys full of bags and tired children.

In mere minutes, they had left the airport building and its air smelling of weary passengers and were outside. India took over: a light breeze wafting with pungent smells of cigarette smoke, car emissions, and soft smells of the earth. Leena smelled perfumes ranging from Dior to Chanel to Dadi's favorite, Charlie, as the well-dressed whizzed past her into the sea of arms of waiting relatives. Grandmothers in saris welcomed the young in *salwaar kameezes*, skirts, shorts, and short shorts. The sea of people grew and receded as waves.

They knew precisely where to stand to greet their visitor and how to break away from the crowd at the right time to head in the direction of the parking lot. Policemen in khaki outfits wandered around, trying to look purposeful and important. As she looked ahead, she could see scores of young men dressed in khaki squatting on the sidewalk beside their black and yellow cabs waiting patiently for passengers.

If you were Suhani, where would you wait?, Leena thought to herself as she fruitlessly scanned the area for a face she did not know.

"Madam, where you going?" the porter stopped talking on his phone for a second and asked Leena.

She fumbled in her purse for the address to her Dadi's relatives as she continued to walk down the pathway out of the airport to the taxi stand.

Then she saw him: a middle-aged man standing at the end of the pathway with a small white board that read "Leena Fresher." "Fresher" made her smile; no one had called her that before but who else could he be looking for. She hesitated for a second. Dadi had mentioned a girl, Suhani, but this was no Suhani.

"Wait, wait, please can you stop," she called out to the porter who was rushing toward a taxi with an open door. The porter stopped and turned around, "What happened, madam? Why no go?"

"Just wait, I have someone here. Please wait."

"Hi, I am Leena Frasher," she smiled weakly at the man holding the board. "You are here for me? I thought Suhani was coming."

"Hi. I am Vinit. You know—your grandma's sister's daughter's son!! Also known as Suhani's husband! Welcome to *amchi Mumbai!* Hot and happening! Of course someone would come to get you—haven't you heard of Indian hospitality? Also my wife would have killed me if I hadn't!" grinned Vinit.

He threw the cigarette he was smoking on the ground and stubbed it out with his expensive-looking leather moccasins. She hesitated for a minute—he seemed genuine enough.

"It is nice to meet you," she smiled. He moved forward to take her well-worn bag from the gangly porter who was busy yapping on his mobile phone and then handed him a brightly colored note in return.

"Just one suitcase? Short visit?"

"Yes, short visit. It is sure hot here," Leena said as the breeze disappeared and the humid weather of Mumbai embraced her, causing her to feel a touch giddy. She wasn't as strong as she used to be. She had run marathons but now a single mile caused her to fall with exhaustion.

"Yes, that is why I call it hot and happening! The hot part you are experiencing and you can see the happening part," he laughed out loud and pointed to the gaggles of young women in outfits that barely covered anything and cigarette smoke that covered everything. "Yes, I can see a lot," she laughed with him.

Leena followed him to his car, taking in all the sights and sounds of the bustling metropolis. The city was wide awake and there were scores of people everywhere walking, talking, in automobiles, motorcycles, cycles, trucks … all busy.

"How far do you live? How long does it take?" she asked as he drove out of the airport.

"Depends on the traffic. If it's a light night we should get there in about a half hour. I can take the scenic route if you are not too tired?" he said and then suddenly jammed the brakes. "Damn these movie stars—do you know Ganesha? He is standing there with his entourage. It is a juice stall that is favored by celebs. Mostly these guys just send their servants or drivers. But sometimes they come and then we get stuck in traffic!"

Leena looked out and barely made out the man's face as he and his troupe got back in the car and drove away. "Isn't he a member of parliament now?" she asked.

"Aren't they all! I am impressed you knew that!!"

"Dadi watches a lot of Indian channels and keeps me updated on these things, regardless of whether I want to hear them or not. She loves Bollywood and all things Bollywood. I know she misses Mumbai. I wish I could have brought her with me but now, at 85, it is hard for her to travel."

"Yes, the flights are long, aren't they? We put a man on the moon and yet cannot invent a plane that crosses oceans in a few hours. Well, I guess the Concorde did that but now it is gone," he continued to chat as he drove.

Leena could see the Arabian Sea in the distance. The roads were buzzing with activity and in spots people were crowded around carts that were selling something.

"What do you do in the States, Leena? Leena, did you fall asleep on me? Come on now, I am not that boring."

"Wow, this place is amazing. Oh, sorry, I work for a small company and handle their accounts … It is really so nice of you all to pick me up and host me, I mean you all barely know me, thank you … "she mumbled.

"Oh, no formality, please. We are family and besides, your Dadi took great care of us when we were kids. We are family!" he said.

When Dadi suggested Leena stay with some unknown relative, Leena had balked at the India-ness of it. "You want me to show up at the doorstep of strangers and ask if I can stay for a few weeks in exchange for nothing, just for being related to them?" "Yes, that is how it is done. You are related by blood. They will welcome you," Dadi had said, beaming with pride, as she sipped her hot chocolate laced with cardamom. The argument had continued for three weeks and judging by the fact that Leena was sitting in Vinit's car in Mumbai, it was clear who had won.

"What … what do you do, Vinit?" Leena inquired.

"Me? I try to look important!" he said disarmingly.

She smiled for the fourth time since meeting him. A record for her.

"I write. I am working on, as Suhani will tell you, yet another unpublishable piece, a true work of genius that only I can see. I keep telling her, just wait—all this practice looking important will pay off someday. I write now. Someday I will be a writer!

"But forget about my unrecognized genius. This is your first time here, right, Leena? Well, there is so much to see and do and so many places to eat. Do you like Italian? There is a great Italian place right there. And oh—do you like the famed Mumbai Burger? Your man, Anthony Bourdain, called our simple *vada pau* a 'Mumbai burger' and it hasn't tasted the same since." He kept talking, not really waiting for her answers. Leena's thoughts of home began to come back and take over. Had Dadi already told him why Leena had really come to Mumbai? She felt the tears welling.

"So, my dear, do tell me, what brings you to Mumbai?" he asked, as if sensing her thoughts.

Either he did not know or was good at pretending.

"Just a short vacation. I, I needed a change. I hope it is not too much of an imposition."

"Don't be silly, it is entirely our pleasure. And speaking of pleasure … we are almost home! Oh, and this must be Suhani," he answered his phone and told his wife they were on their way and would be arriving in a few minutes.

Vinit and his family lived in a two-bedroom apartment in the highly utilitarian area of Mahim. The suburb smelled of everyday life with all its sweetness and all its bitterness. The crowds thinned as he navigated his car into smaller roadways and alleys. The quiet building was the side of a long, main road lined with other small towers and tiny bungalows.

Vinit pulled up to the small building and a night watchman opened the main gate. "Every building here has a watchman so that the riffraff don't come in and sleep on the stairs like in that *Death of Vishnu* book. Good book, but I don't want to come home to my flat at two in the morning to see a Vishnu on my steps," he grinned. Leena knew the book, written by a local college professor in Maryland, was a huge success. She owned an autographed copy.

"Is your book going to be like the *Vishnu* book?" she asked as he deftly parked the small Maruti car in a spot that seemed too small for even a motorcycle.

"Don't get me started on my writing right now or Suhani will not let us into the house."

They walked up the stairs to the apartment on the third floor. After the loud noises at the airport, this building was peaceful. A golden haze from a single bulb fell on the stairs of the building.

Suddenly a door opened and a petite, pony-tailed woman dressed in black jogging pants and a black t-shirt that read BEBE smiled at them.

"Welcome. Welcome. I am Suhani. I am so glad Vinit did not scare you enough to take the same flight back to the US. How was your flight? You look just like your father!"

She extended a hand and pulled Leena inside and gave her a big hug.

Vinit brought in Leena's bag and placed it by the side of the door.

A bronze solider statue sat at the left side of the entrance. The sparsely furnished room sparkled under the tube lights. Leena guessed that she had entered what her Dadi told her was called a drawing room or main hall in Indian homes. The room held two small white futon-like couches, a center table with an emerald-green vase full of fresh flowers, and a large picture window that was dark as night. Playful touches were everywhere—a small doll wearing an ethnic skirt and holding a book was next to the flowers. The walls were full of shelves backed with lighted mirrors. The large bowls on the shelves attracted Leena's eye. They glittered with stones of various kinds. A local newscast appeared to flicker on the flat-screen TV mounted on the center wall of the room. The room was chilly as the AC on full blast attempted to battle the heat of the season.

The house was a home.

Leena moved toward the futon, her legs ached, and her back throbbed. Her exhaustion drained her tiny reserves of strength and energy.

Just as she was about to sit down, Suhani piped up, "Oh wait, don't settle down yet. We have to go back out. Did you not hear the news? The water of the Arabian Sea has become sweet! Everyone is headed that way, including many of the celebs. Come on, we have to go and see what is going on."

Both Leena and Vinit looked at her, totally puzzled. Suhani took the TV off mute and pointed to the screen.

"What? You guys did not notice the crowds on your way here? Look, it is on TV. *News Today* is reporting that the ocean water has become sweet. Look at the crowds. See … people are drinking it. Look, look," she said. There were swarms of people standing on the beaches, using their cupped hands to drink the ocean water. A young reporter was sticking her microphone into random faces asking them if the water really was sweet. The camera then panned over to a holy man, wearing a saffron robe and large beads, declaring God was coming back to earth as He had made the salt water sweet.

Vinit walked over to her and took the remote from her hand and muted the sound again.

"Suhani, the people drinking that water are going to get sick. That sea water is so polluted with sewage and garbage. This sounds like a load of crap. I cannot believe you want to go there?!"

"Indians must have a more benevolent God," said Leena quietly.

"Yes, that and a full-time propaganda machine called twenty-four-hour news," he remarked, and gave his wife a sharp look.

"I guess you are right. I am just being silly about the whole thing," Suhani said responding to the look her husband gave her.

Then reluctantly she turned the TV off.

"I am so sorry to be rude, Leena. Welcome, welcome. Come and sit with me. I am so glad to meet you. Sorry, I just got carried away. Oh, you look exhausted. What will you have to drink—*kya peyoge*? I am so sorry, do you understand Hindi? Here I am ready to drag you back out after such a long flight. I am so sorry." The questions Suhani asked had no requirements for answers, just like her husband's chatter earlier. As abruptly as she had sat down, she stood up and disappeared into the depth of the house and returned instantly with a cold bottle of spring water.

"I know people who come from the States worry about the water here. It isn't so bad but on your first few days, drink this. Of course, if you would prefer to try the sweet sea water, we can go there now."

They all laughed.

Leena gulped it greedily, the cool liquid providing much needed relief.

"How is your Dadi? I spoke to her this morning. She sounds rather frail now." Suhani wanted to know as Vinit disappeared into one of the inner rooms.

"She is fine. She remembers you a lot. Thanks so much for letting me visit. The past few weeks have been …," Leena responded.

"It is our pleasure Leena. Your Dadi told me that your cancer is now in remission. Don't even think about all that now. Stay as long as you need. Mumbai is a great place to recover—it is a city with a life of its own and its fun spirit will take you in and never let go. You will meet Avni tomorrow," said Suhani getting up off the couch.

"Who is Avni? Pretty name. Does it mean something special?"

"It means 'the earth.' I should have named her Agni, the fire. She is my devil child. Looks like a movie star and thinks she can rule the world," Suhani's eyes twinkled as she gracefully picked up Leena's handbag and moved it into the tiny room that seemed to be the guest room, laundry room, reading room, and general storage room all in one.

"Good night," Vinit popped his head in. "Just rest. We will have lots of time to catch up tomorrow."

Twenty hours on the plane was twenty hours too many. Leena debated taking a shower but in the end the inviting bed won. Sleep had not been her friend. Yet tonight it hugged her like a forbidden lover, soothing her, holding her, and inviting her to relinquish all control and just slip into its pleasurable arms.

"You are the meanest mother EVER," screamed a young voice. The sound jolted Leena out of her deep sleep.

She could hear heated female voices outside her door and the sounds of an incessantly ringing doorbell, followed by distinct voices speaking various languages.

"You are committing adultery," Suhani was screaming.

"It is called fornication, mother. It is only adultery when people are married."

Ah, so this was Avni.

Dadi would have a coronary, Leena thought, *if I ever spoke to her like this. Suhani was right, Avni should have been Agni, the fire.*

"You and dad tried swinging, didn't you? Don't bother denying it. I heard you talk about it with my own ears. If you can do it and it's not adultery, why are you getting mad at me for going out with Salil? I love him. We want to get married. I am seventeen. You cannot tell me what to do."

"We are *not* swingers, Avni. Don't talk nonsense. You are such a devil, sometimes, child. I just don't know what to do with you." A few doors banged and then there was silence.

Unsure of what to do next, Leena sat on the bed for some time. The room had only one small window, but it quickly filled the room with the bright Mumbai sun. She opened her bag and decided the easiest, most painless thing would be to brush her teeth and shower. And then decide what to do for her two totally unplanned weeks in Mumbai.

Suhani was waiting with breakfast at the small breakfast table in the living room when Leena emerged from the bathroom. "I made you some toast. Hope that is okay? Do you like instant coffee or shall I make you some tea? Tea? Great. *Bai*, this way, this way … please clean this side," the instructions for Leena and the cleaning lady coming all together.

"So what happened to the sweet sea water?" Leena asked recalling the crazy night. "Ah, that, well apparently there is a scientific explanation … something about too much rain, I did not hear the whole thing. I sort of lost interest in it once they said it is not a miracle. Here is the paper if you want to read it," Suhani smiled, her dimpled smile reminding Leena of her own mother. It had a peaceful yet very playful quality about it.

"I just want to let you know that you are welcome to stay as long as you wish. Here in Mumbai the space is tight but our hearts are big! I know everyone says that but I mean it. Stay as long as you like, okay? Vinit told me that you were thanking him and all. No need for such formality. This is your home, okay?" Suhani leaned over and kissed Leena on the forehead.

Leena felt her body relax and her breathing became quiet and steady. Perhaps her Dadi was right. A new place would do her good.

She greedily gobbled down the toast and the ginger tea.

"So when do I get to meet Avni, Suhani?" Leena asked with a big smile on her face. She couldn't wait to meet the young firecracker.

"Oh, she left this morning in one of her moods. You will meet her at dinner this evening, assuming she decides to grace us with her presence. She is like that. Oh these teenagers. All my hair will turn white before she hits eighteen," Suhani said, and disappeared into the kitchen with yet another servant, and then came out and went into the guest room, giving the cleaning lady detailed instructions on how to sweep, where to sweep and where not to sweep … all in one breath.

Leena placed her plate and cup into the tiny steel sink in the kitchen and began to rinse it.

"Don't drink that tap water or you will get sick," boomed Suhani's voice from the other room, "I have placed bottled water for you in the fridge." Leena smiled—all moms somehow manage to give the illusion of knowing it all at the same time, and being everywhere at the same time.

She walked into the living room and looked outside the window onto the awakening streets of Mumbai outside. Young people vividly dressed in Indian clothing, young women with their dark, long hair in braids, were walking with books in hand toward a college building located a stone's throw from the apartment. Buses were zooming. Cars of every shape and size alongside bicycles, scooters, bullock carts, pedestrians, and motorcycles zipped up and down. A man selling vegetables from a pushcart appeared to be arguing heatedly on his phone and also with a lady picking vegetables from his cart. The discussion was loud yet neither seemed fazed.

Across the street, Leena saw a young lady standing by a window in a building. The woman was picking something off a plate that she was holding and throwing it onto the street.

"We Indians love to do that," Vinit said as he came up behind her, "Throw our trash on the street. See, she is picking out stones from her rice. She won't throw it in a trashcan but out on the road. You will see her later, throwing her whole garbage out the same window. Pathetic, really."

"You are too funny. You know, I remember my mother would do this and Papa always teased her because he said there were no stones in the rice in the US but she continued to do it for years," replied Leena.

"Do you know what you would like to do today? You can come with me if you like or if you are still jet lagging you can nap, or if you want to go to the happening part of Mumbai you can go with Suhani to her kitty party today," Vinit said.

"Where are you heading? But also, what is a kitty party?" she asked.

"Oh, come with me to my kitty, I will introduce you to my friends! We all pool in money in a kitty and get together, over a lunch of course, to see who wins the kitty for the month! I am in several of them. Come, come, the girls will love to meet you!" Suhani joined in the discussion from the kitchen.

Leena looked questioningly at Vinit.

"Forget her kitty, come with me. I am writing love stories about temple prostitutes," he winked.

"Temple prostitutes? How was that possible? Temples have prostitutes? You are teasing me because I don't know India well?" Leena said.

"See—this is what I tell Suhani constantly. This is India: for every logical thing, the exact opposite will also be true! It is a big world out there and letting it in will let you open your soul a bit.

"You see, I am working on a story about *devadasis*—the Temple Dancers. They are also called the servants of Gods— they were trained dancers who danced simply for themselves in temples. It was an amazing and beautiful tradition. They had patrons and they lived well. But then, it all changed. Sadly, they became prostitutes when hard times hit, it all started when the colonizers came ...," he explained.

"Stop, Vinit, you will bore her to death with all your history. Let her be," Suhani shouted from the kitchen.

"Come with me. I am going to a temple in Borivali where a devadasi, a temple dancer, from Karnataka has taken refuge. I will show you."

Suhani came out of the kitchen, "I heard all that. Leena, you don't have to go if you don't want to. Vinit, it is her first day in Mumbai—how about we take her to Gate of India or show her the sights and sounds of the city instead of your decrepit structures? He loves to spend all this time at that broken-down building that once *used to be* a temple. He and his crazy friend Sunny seem to think it is still inhabited by the spirits of some dancers. And you think I am nuts for wanting to try the sweet water."

Leena laughed. She loved the friendly dynamic between the husband and wife.

"I think I will try the temple, if you don't mind. It sounds interesting," she said.

"Well, don't say I did not warn you! And remind him to feed himself and you. Or he will forget!" Suhani smiled as she walked over and held her husband's hand.

Within a few minutes both Leena and Vinit were ready to go.

"I gave the driver the day off today so I am driving," Vinit told Leena as they got into the car.

The car ride to the temple offered Leena the opportunity to watch the city in its morning glory. It was around eleven in the morning and Mumbai was wide awake, even more so than the previous night at the airport. The drive, Vinit had told her, was going to take over an hour. They passed high-rise buildings rivaling those Leena had seen in New York City and areas of slums that she had never seen anywhere.

"Vinit, there … that kid … he has no clothes and still he is smiling and playing. How is that?" Leena asked as she pointed out her window to a child playing on the sidewalk.

"Happiness is free," he said.

They reached the old temple driving at a leisurely place through winding roads and small lanes. Vinit kept his commentary about his work going and Leena found his soothing tone and gentle words evoking a lullaby-like effect in a strange land.

"You really don't talk much, do you?" Vinit teased her.

"Oh, no, sorry. I was just enjoying listening to you," Leena said. But she knew he was right. Dadi made those comments about her constantly, "Leena, beta, you have to come out of this shell. You have to talk. How long are you going to keep everything bottled inside?" Leena would just hug her and cry.

The temple came into view as they turned into a small, rough, sandy path. "See—it is barely a shadow of its original magnificent self," Vinit kept explaining. It was a cheerless building; its walls showing clear signs of neglect, old age, and the results of the incessant beating down of the monsoon rains.

They parked the car and walked up to the building. The dusty, carved walls showed remnants of beautiful intricate carvings of dancers and various Hindu Gods—noses, breasts, hands had all fallen off, making the carvings look macabre and limbless. A set of broken and unstable stairs led into a courtyard that housed flowers, still in full bloom.

"Who cares for these pretty flowers?" she asked.

Vinit pointed to an old lady walking at the other end of the temple. Wearing a dark blue cotton sari, she had her head covered and was scurrying around carrying something. She looked up and saw them and then hid her face from them with her crumpled sari. She moved closer to the walls of the temple, as though hoping to get absorbed in its shadows and crevices.

"She is the last remaining devadasi here. She lives here and looks after this place. She was 'donated' to a temple in the south when she was about eight. She lived there until she was seventy and then moved here about fifteen years ago. She thinks she was given to the temple in exchange for her parents' wish for a son. She was supposed to be like the bride of God and learn dancing and fine arts," he said.

"Sounds a bit like the geisha culture in Japan," replied Leena.

"Well—sort of. But this tradition was supposed to have a religious backing. Sometimes she talks to me, and her stories are sad but amazing—she tells me that once she entered puberty, there was no more money at the temple and all the priests left. She was there alone. There was no one to shield her from the world. A woman who took care of the temple grounds sold her to anyone who wanted to sleep with her ... often six to seven men a day."

"What? That is rape ... she was a minor," Leena interjected.

"I know. It is heartbreaking. She is such a nice lady but all, all shriveled up inside and out. It is like someone squeezed the spirit out of her and now this thing of bones and blood wanders around here, watering these stupid flowers."

"Vinit, I don't understand this. Why did she not run away, why was she still here?" asked Leena as they walked towards a small bench. She guessed that he had sensed her need to sit due to her weak body.

"Run away and go where, Leena? Come sit here with me." he said. "Now, think it about it—back then there was nowhere for them to go and start a new life. No money, no transport. They lived the hand they were dealt. These days there is hope of escape and a better life for the newer recruits. But her? She says she has two sons who left as soon as they understood what she did. Now she can barely see and barely walk. Tell me where will she go and who will take care of her? Familiarity provides comfort and no one bothers her here."

He got up to go see if she would speak to him, leaving Leena on the bench.

Leena was stunned. Eighty years of prostitution in this place, in this serene scene. Surrounded by giant green trees, the temple, a temple only in name, almost seemed to be an island all its own. It was just an old building with some carvings. There is no way this place could have a title as holy as "temple." The leaves rustled quietly as a gentle, cool breeze blew all around. The air smelled of jasmine, sweet and fragrant.

Vinit returned a few minutes later, "She won't talk today, so let's just go inside. Are you okay? Do you need a drink?"

"I am fine. This is as sad as it is fascinating."

"Please tell Suhani that. She thinks I am torturing you by bringing you here and not taking to you the Mumbai tourist traps. She has SMSed me ten times already to bring you back home," he said, laughing.

As they entered the main temple room, her eyes were drawn to the exotic paintings, or what remained of them, on the temple walls. She noticed a young man standing beside them. He had a notepad in hand and was staring intently at the drawings.

"Hey … Sunny, you are here already? Come here, let me introduce you," Vinit called out to him.

The young man turned around and smiled; Leena had to catch her breath. Sundeep Suri—or Sunny as his friends like to call him—was tall, with dark hair softly falling over his forehead, a lanky frame and light brown eyes. He seemed, to her, like a young George Clooney. He wore a white t-shirt that read, KISS ME, I AM PUNJABI. It made Leena laugh out loud.

"Sunny," said Vinit, walking up toward him, "meet Leena. She is visiting from the big, bad US of A. Leena, this is my *yaar,* the one and only Dr. Sundeep Suri."

"Hey, it is nice to meet you," Sunny's deep voice perfectly matched his physique. Leena held out her hand.

"Nice to meet you as well. You are a doctor? Not a writer?" she said pointing to his note pad.

"No, no," Vinit laughed and said before Sunny could respond. "He is the real thing. He only hangs out with me at Suhani's request. She sends him here to make sure I go back home in the evenings! He is what they call in India a lady's doctor, or what you would call an OB/GYN."

"I am an ex-doctor, actually," Sunny interrupted, "I don't practice any more. Now I illustrate Vinit's books."

"Oh, don't bore her with your droning," laughed Vinit. "Leena, he is being too humble. He is a terrible doctor and no woman wants to be near him so he had to quit! But he does run a library. I will take you there one day. Anyway, I have an SMS from Suhani that we need to eat and to feed you. You must be famished!"

Leena had forgotten about food. The mere mention of it made her realize how hungry she was, and all of a sudden, she needed to sit down. A bit of dizziness combined with the jet lag was still making her feel a bit out of sorts.

"She needs a drink, Vinit. Be right back," and Sunny was gone.

He came back a few minutes later with a Limca, a fizzy, lemony drink. "Here, drink this and then let's go get a bite."

"I will leave my bike here and come with you and then you drop me back here so I can finish up the last few pages," Sunny said to Vinit.

They got in the car and headed to a small South Indian joint a few minutes away from the temple. Although Leena was fascinated with the world outside, the fascination was even more so with the world inside the car.

"Did she talk to you today?" Sunny asked.

"No, she seems even more subdued than usual. Something must have happened," he answered as he maneuvered the car around the flocks of people on the tiny cramped streets.

"So tell me more about this tradition, why would these girls do this?" Leena asked.

"It is not a question of choice. In the olden days, you know, this was a very respected profession. They were dancers, kings would marry them and give them homes and money. Then—and India has a crazy history—when the British came and the kings lost power, these women, who were artists, were demoted to the title of 'dancing girls' like the ones you see in cheap bars," Sunny explained.

"So they just turned into prostitutes?" Leena asked.

"Well, no one turns into a prostitute. Many died in poverty, some were forced into prostitution to make a living, some stayed, some tried to run away. Anyway, that is what we are working on. It is a sad part of our history that no one is capturing," Vinit added.

"So let's move off this for a minute at least. Leena, where are you visiting from in the US? Are you here on work or pleasure? And if you say pleasure I have to ask what the hell you are doing with Vinit?" Sunny asked lightening the mood in the car from serious to amusing.

"Oh, too funny. I live in DC. I think I visited India when I was about three or four with my father, he was related to Vinit's family, but I haven't been back here since."

"So in reality this is your first REAL visit? And Vinit, you idiot, you brought her here instead of taking her to see some nice Mumbai sights? And now she is going to eat at this roadside place with us? Oh, oh … please forgive my friend," Sunny said.

"It is her first day here, dude, first day and she chose to come with me. I told her about Suhani and her kitties but Leena likes me! What can I say?" Vinit chuckled.

"So what brings you here, Leena? Sightseeing? Work? Yoga?" Sunny asked.

"Well, just needing a break I guess. My Dadi thought it would be good for me to come explore the city were my father grew up," Leena fidgeted in her seat. Okay, so it was partly true.

They arrived at the tiny eatery.

"Don't worry, this will not give you Delhi belly! It is tried and tested!" exclaimed Vinit as he led her into the small but clean eatery with ten tables and a handful of chairs.

"Vinit, sir! Happy you are back and you have a new friend," a young man in jeans and a cut-off white t-shirt approached them from behind the cash counter.

"Anil—meet Leena. Leena, Anil is a model but also helps run this place for his father. Anil, Leena is just down from the States and this is her first meal here. Make it good!"

"Welcome, Leena! This place may look a little, how shall I say, well … down-market but I can tell you, the food is excellent! I will get you all started with dosas," Anil shook her hand and then disappeared back into the tiny kitchen.

"So now, it is my turn to ask the questions. You are an ex-doctor?" Leena asked Sunny. "What exactly is an ex-doc? I know doctors retire but you don't look quite at the retirement age yet."

"Let's just say that I wasn't cut out to be a physician, shall we?" Sunny smiled.

"Oh, come on. Now I feel like there is juicy gossip you are not sharing," Leena said as she tore a piece of the crisp lentil and rice dosa placed in front of her and dipped it into the steaming bowl of lentils.

"During his doctoring days, Sunny here discovered the dark side of India first-hand," Vinit said as he tore a piece of his dosa and used the piece to scoop up the spiced, mashed potatoes nestled inside the dosa.

"Oh, I am sorry, I did not mean to pry. If you don't want to talk about it, that is fine. I was just asking," she said.

"No, no, you are not prying. It was a fair question. I was practicing in a remote area of Punjab. It was my first year, I had just finished med school and thought I would go to the villages and help out ... But there was something a little off there and I could not figure out what ..."

"How so?"

"Something just did not feel right. I was assigned to a tiny clinic. I don't know how it is in the US, but in India, especially in these tiny villages, most women don't really go to doctors. And if they do, they definitely do not go to male docs. Anyway, the school I was with set me up here. And then what set off my initial suspicion was that pregnant women would show up with their husbands to see me ... I know that is fairly common in the US but here pregnancy is still a very private, very womanly issue and especially in villages, the women are still shy about it. I would have thought they would come with their mothers or mothers-in-law. I even asked the doctor I was working with and he just said that maybe it is because I am a man that they are coming with a man. We could do no physical exams, only talk to them and take their vitals."

"Yes, I remember even when Suhani was pregnant with Avni, she preferred going to the doctor with her mother. Heck, I was not even allowed inside when the baby was delivered, she wanted her mom," Vinit added.

"How is the dosa, friends? I am sending out the *thali* next, okay?" Anil yelled from behind the cash counter. Both Sunny and Vinit gave him a thumbs up.

"It took a few months for me to realize that the men were coming to make sure they knew the sex of the baby. They did not want daughters," Sunny said as he pushed aside his dosa. His eyes narrowed and Leena could see that whatever had happened still haunted him.

"Really, it's okay if you would rather not talk about it," she said regretting her decision to ask earlier.

"It is life. I figured out they were coming to ask me the sex of the baby and when I told them that legally I could not tell them, I found out that they resorted to old wives' tales—if the mother was eating sweets or carrying the baby in a certain way, they presumed it was a girl. And do you know how I found out? My nurse told me that women were coming in with their privates burned with acid. They wanted to abort and thought the acid would do it."

Leena shuddered and stopped eating.

He continued. "Then it started to get even stranger. Around twenty weeks of pregnancy, I would send them for ultrasounds to confirm the anatomical growth of the baby. But then many would not come back for delivery. I kept wondering what was going on, but the head of the clinic told me either they had miscarriages or changed doctors."

"Are you sure you want to hear the rest of it, Leena? You just got here and we don't want you to give you the worst side of India on your first day," Vinit's eyes had narrowed and his jovial demeanor was gone.

"Please, do share, I am fine," she replied.

Sunny continued, "One evening, I came in late to the clinic because I had forgotten my mobile. The old woman, a *diae*, you know—I think they are called midwives in the US—was sitting by a dried-up well near the clinic and crying. The stench around her was unbelievable. We had been told at the clinic that the stench was from some farm animals that had died in the farm behind the clinic. I guess I was naïve, I believed them."

Sunny's voice trailed off. Their table was quiet except for the noise from the other tables that seemed to rudely infiltrate the miserable moment. His next few sentences were a confirmation that he had found hell on earth. The *daie* had pointed to the well. He had walked over and looked in, a decision he regretted till today. At first he could not see anything. The well appeared to be dry. The old lady came up behind him and shone her oil lantern over the well. Sunny turned around and threw up. Baby corpses, fetuses that appeared to be aborted halfway through the pregnancy, and bones ... baby bones, what seemed to be a mountain of them were in the well. "*Kudiya ... manu maaff kar deo, rabaa.* Girls forgive me," the *daie* had begun to wail louder. These were the girls, these were the deliveries he never saw. Turns out, the clinic's ultrasound technician was being paid by the husbands, and even some of the women, to reveal the sex of the babies.

"That was it, I left and never went back. There seemed to be no point. I knew the owners were involved. I felt there was nothing I could do. I came here about a year ago and met Vinit at a bookstore. We have been friends since."

Leena's eyes filled with tears.

"I did not mean to depress you on your first day out, I apologize," Sunny said.

"No, no, you did not. Just makes me realize how big the world is and how little I know about it."

They ate steamed rice generously topped with tempered yellow lentils and sipped cold orange-flavored Fanta, quietly, and then dropped Sunny back to the temple and Leena and Vinit returned to the apartment.

"I feel like the room is spinning," Leena said as they entered the apartment. Suhani helped her to bed. "Just rest. You will be fine tomorrow. I will check in on you at dinner. If you are still sleeping, we will let you be."

The next morning, Leena met Avni at breakfast. The young woman, with her chiseled features, flowing dark hair and radiant smile, looked older than her young seventeen years.

"Hi! Mama told me you were here, sorry I haven't even met you yet! So what brings you to Desiland, Leena *Di*?" she asked as she sat at the breakfast table drinking a can of Coke.

"Just a visit. I thought I would explore the city," Leena replied.

"Mama tells me that Papa dragged you to his temple thing yesterday? How about today you hang with me and I will show you the fun side of Mumbai?" Avni grinned and winked at Leena.

"I would love that. I am still feeling a bit tired. How about we start with a walk around your area? I feel like I just want to see this place first before even wandering into the city!"

"So you are not coming with me today?" Vinit joined them at the table. "I hope it is not because of the discussion about the village."

"Vinit!" Suhani shrieked from the kitchen. "You did not tell her about Sunny, did you? Prostitution, feticide, oh, my ... Leena, what will you think of us ... We are good. Just that there are dark sides."

"I know. I know. There are dark sides everywhere. Besides, I am really just tired. I don't have my strength ... "Leena's voice trailed off as she realized she was about to step into a subject she did not want to talk about just yet.

"Then, come on, let's go out now. It is gorgeous outside and not hot yet," Avni got up, threw her can in the trashcan and waited for Leena to get ready.

For the next several days, Leena rested at home in the morning. Dadi had been texting her every day, several times a day. "I am fine, Dadi, really. These people really surprise me.

They don't push me to do anything I don't want to do and just let me be. I hope I don't overstay my welcome. I am beginning to really love it here."

After restful days, in the evenings Leena went for long walks in the small, ill-manicured park behind the apartment. It was a tiny park with tiny pathways built for walkers. Although it was not well cared for, there were gorgeous red roses in bloom and she loved to stop by and smell them each evening.

Avni accompanied her each time. They walked and talked for hours. Well, mostly Avni talked about her boyfriend, their love-life, her mother not understanding true love, and Leena listened. She enjoyed the youthfulness and naïveté of this young Indian girl trying to grow up in the throes of a traditional culture wrenching itself toward a seemingly more modern world. It was so different from her own life entrenched deep in cancer-fighting days and deep, depression-filled demonic nights. Avni was a breath of fresh air, totally in love with life and its offerings. She laughed at everything, smiled constantly, and held nothing back when it came to her opinions.

To Leena's immense pleasure, Sunny dropped in a few times. While he and Vinit would work on their book while seated in the dining room, she would listen in and just watch him. She would catch him stealing glances at her while pretending to listen to Vinit reading his passionate notes on their book.

"Leena, di, you like him, don't you?" Avni asked her one evening on a walk.

"I do not."

"You do. I did not even tell you whom I was talking about. But di, seriously, for a guy to notice you, you have to get out of these damn jeans and these dark t-shirts. Come on, this is India, let me get you into some vibrant colors. You know, Mama is dying to take you shopping," Avni teased.

At first, Leena resisted, conscious of her lack of breasts.

"You may lose a breast, but the cancer will be out forever," her Dadi had said when convincing her, last year, to go for a total mastectomy at twenty-one.

"I look fine. Please, I don't want to talk about looks. I look fine," Leena pleaded to Avni in a quiet voice.

"No, you don't. I have never met someone who is so bent on looking out of place and hiding their God-given beauty. Come on, we need to add some zing to your wardrobe."

In a day, gone were the jeans and the dark shirt, replaced by colorful skirts, silk blouses, bangles, anklets, and even makeup. Leena was surprised at herself. She felt like a new person, just with a change of clothes.

Avni roped in Suhani, who was more than happy to buy Leena new clothes and jewelry to add to her new style.

"You have to let me pay for these," Leena insisted.

"Really, if I was your mother, which by the way I am old enough to be, would you even dare utter those words? Rubbish. Just enjoy. You look glorious," Suhani kissed Leena's forehead as they left the mall with their enormous shopping bags.

Vinit commented, "*Mumbai tumko jum gai* as they say here, Mumbai suits you, you are glowing, Leena."

Even Sunny noticed. "What happened to your dark shirts? You are beaming in these colors, by the way."

Before Leena could say anything she felt a sting in her buttock. Avni pinched her and gave her an "I told you so" look.

The next morning, Leena approached Vinit and Suhani at the breakfast table, "I think I am ready to see the city now! Do you have any recommendations of tour companies?"

"Tour companies? Are you kidding? Sunny has been asking me for the past three days how to ask you if he can show you the city. Shall I call him for you?"

Leena felt a warmth rise in her cheeks. "Vinit, the girl is blushing! Just call him," Suhani added.

"You are stealing my partner, Leena," Vinit complained good-naturedly as he called Sunny on his phone.

With that one phone call that lasted all of thirty seconds, Leena and Sunny became inseparable—he took her for morning walks at the Maha Laksmi racecourse, lunch at the Taj, and then Victoria rides during the cool Mumbai evenings. They visited every tourist spot in town and his knowledge of the city kept her interested and enticed. He loved seafood and soon had her walking with him in area fish markets to pick out fresh fish that he then cleaned and cooked for her in simmering sauces of coconut milk, red peppers, and tamarind. Somewhere during the time they spent together, Leena could not recall which day it happened: she held his hand for the first time. Now it was a habit.

Vinit did steal Sunny on some days to finish the illustrations for the book. On those evenings, Leena would look forward to her walks with Avni, although she did notice that their walks included a lot of sitting down! They sat on the ratty, old wooden park benches and watched the kids from Avni's building play cricket. She could never tell who won but the kids seemed not to care. No parents were ever in sight watching the kids, something that really surprised Leena.

"We are supposed to be all about community here, watching each other. Most people do it because they are nosy," joked Avni, "some even care. I could never imagine my parents coming to watch me when I played. It is just not done here."

"Come on, *arre*, throw the ball, what are you doing?" The kids' yells were constant.

Across from the bench where they sat was an old man with a red bandana-type wrap around his head and a clean white shirt, who had a small parrot. Avni had told her that the man claimed his parrot could read fortunes. One day, when she was on her own, Leena went up to him to have her fortune read. "Madam, *appki maa kahti hai sub teek hoga.*" Leena had no idea what he was saying so she called one of the boys playing cricket. A group of them came running up. "*Didi*, we can translate. He is saying—your mother says that all will be well …" The kids then ran off. Leena thanked the old man and paid him a hundred rupees, much to his gratitude, and went back to her bench. Her mother and father had died hiking in the Virginia mountains about two years ago, and then came the devastating breast cancer diagnosis. Life had been anything but dull.

The past ten days had been strangely liberating, all the emotional baggage left behind in DC. Tania had finally called on the tenth day. "Dadi will only text you now because she cannot hear anything you are saying on the phone," Tania's melodious voice made Leena long to go back.

She told Tania that she was now an expert in bargaining and bargain hunting.

"You sound so different, Leena, so much happier and I loved all your new clothes in the photos you emailed me. What are you buying for me? I want to come visit and stay with Avni. She sounds so wonderful. And Leena, who is that handsome guy in the photos? The one wearing the t-shirt that says NEVER, NEVER, NEVER HAVE A BAD DAY?" Tania asked.

Ah, yes, the t-shirt. Only one person had the disposition to wear that. Sunny.

"His name is Sunny, he is a young Punjabi guy here. He makes me laugh so much, Tania, I don't know how this man constantly finds something to be happy about," Leena told her sister.

"Leena, I love you. I feel like you are becoming your old self again. I miss you. Come home," Tania cried at the end of the call.

Leena wiped away her own tears. Suhani sat down next to her.

"You miss your family, I know. I hope this break has been good for you, my sweet child," Suhani said gently moving her fingers through Leena's hair.

"Yes, I feel much more at peace. It has been a difficult road. I, me ... when I lost my breasts, I thought my life would be over."

Before Suhani could respond, the maid brought over some tea and onion fritters for the ladies to enjoy.

"So listen, what made you think Sunny is Punjabi? I overheard you on the phone," Suhani said as she sipped her tea.

"Oh, I just assumed, from that t-shirt he always wears— KISS ME I AM PUNJABI. He never really shares anything about his family. Our conversations mostly revolve around things like the taxi drivers of Mumbai or the people peeing on the side of the road, the road-pee kings, as he calls them."

"Oh, that t-shirt. No, no, he isn't Punjabi. I don't think he even knows where he is from. He generally does not share his strange past, Leena. As far as I know he was on the streets of Delhi when some Mumbai socialite found him. She sent him to boarding school and paid for his education. When he was younger, I think he grew up either in her house or in an orphanage. He won't say. When he was in medical college he fell in love with a young Punjabi girl. Vinit told me she was the love of his life. She told him that his demeanor, laughter, and yes, his fair-skinned good looks reminded her of all her Punjabi friends in Delhi. He had that t-shirt printed up the next day."

Leena stopped sipping her tea. Nothing here was as it seemed. Nothing.

"I cannot believe it. He, he ... well, he behaves like he has it all. Everything. Wanting for nothing," she said quietly.

It was true, she had seen him serious only that first day when she met him. After that, he was always cheery and like many people she saw on Mumbai streets, appeared to follow Vinit's "happiness is free" paradigm.

"I know. I envy him, too. Have you ever seen that library of his? No? What! You guys go out all the time and he hasn't taken you to his library?? Come on … at least I know part of where he gets his strength from." Suhani left her tea, picked up her purse and was already halfway out the door.

Leena fumbled around for her purse and then followed.

They hailed a taxi and within twenty minutes were outside an old, broken down house.

"He lives here as a paying guest with a Parsi family. His room and library are in the back of the house," Suhani said as she pointed to a small bungalow. She paid the taxi driver and began walking toward the small house. They walked by a small, well-tended patch with tiny yellow roses in full bloom. Sweet-smelling jasmine grew freely outside the right side of the house leading to the back. No one appeared to be home. Then they heard the laughter. Sunny was outside in the tiny garden surrounded by little kids and was playing ball with them.

"Hey. What a surprise, ladies! So nice to see you! Welcome to my humble abode," he waved to them.

"Hi, Sunny! Suhani finally decided to show me what you have been hiding from me all these days," Leena teased.

"Sunny—show her where your library is, and please get me something to drink. I am so hot," said Suhani.

"Come, come let me get you something to drink. Library? Yes, of course, … here it is," he said pointing to a small, shabbily built shack. The shelves of the shed were filled with toys of every kind. "This is where my money goes—my, ahem, my toy library. And now people donate. These little ones, who no one really gives a damn about, come here to play." The little kids, dressed in tattered clothes, giggled and laughed as a brightly dressed toy monkey banged on his drums and waddled forward.

"They are orphans?" Leena asked, instantly regretting the biased question.

"No, not all of them. Some have parents. But they are all, well, poor. No money. My library allows them to play. People often donate clothes and foods to these kids, forgetting that they are kids. They too have the right to play. To be happy, to laugh, and to smile. They have a right," his voice trailed off as a young child came over and pulled him to complain about a toy not working.

He bent down to the child's level and became immersed in fixing the toy. Leena walked over and sat by Suhani.

"I have never heard of a toy library. What a unique idea."

"He is like the Pied Piper, isn't he," Suhani said, her eyes misting. "They love him. This is what I was telling you. I think this is his secret—he gets his strength from them."

They sat for a while on old white lawn chairs and watched, a bit in awe and a bit in envy, as Sunny effortlessly interacted with the kids. He had a large jug of juice and a bowl filled with grapes and peeled oranges. As he played with the kids, he would motion for them to get something to eat or drink.

About an hour or so later, the sky began to darken. The kids left. Sunny came over and sat down. "I am sorry but I promise them that I will play with them when they are here. I did not mean to ignore you guys! I love them, you know. I hope I can encourage at least one to go to school. Right now they are so busy being kids that I hate to even mention the future.

"So, what are you ladies up to tonight? Have you been to Enigma yet, Leena? Wanna go dancing?" He was full of surprises, Leena had no idea he liked to go bar hopping or dancing.

Suhani called Vinit on his mobile. Avni was at her friend's house spending the night, so they were all free to head out. "Yes, sounds fun. We will meet you at Enigma at around ten?" Suhani and Leena left to go back to the apartment to have dinner and get ready. Leena caught Sunny staring quietly at the toys sprawled across the garden. He was smiling.

I am falling in love with this man, she thought and then her hands self-consciously reached for her chest. She brushed the thoughts of her disfigured body out of her mind and tried to keep up with Suhani who was already in a taxi, negotiating the rate to take them back home. At least that is what Leena thought.

"We are not going home," announced Suhani. "Come on, we are going to get our hair done, manicures, pedicures, waxing and maybe even a massage. I have to shine for my hubby this evening. Enigma has women half my age." She was smiling.

Leena was thrilled and nervous, the prospect of getting all dolled up for no special reason sounded like some much needed pampering. At the salon, she got her hair done and her nails painted a bright red.

Their tall hairdresser with a wild mohawk and bright fuchsia lipstick named "Pinky" continuously referred to each one of them as "Baby."

"We have been taking bets for years on Pinky's P's, care to join in?" laughed Suhani when the hairdresser was out of earshot.

"P's?"

"Privates," whispered Suhani and they both giggled.

At home, Suhani helped her pick out a sizzling red top from Avni's closet and paired it with a pair of black jeans. "You will break a lot of hearts this evening, you look amazing!" Suhani exclaimed after Leena finished dressing.

That night was a blur. It was a loud, hip bar with fusion music blaring from umpteen speakers. The dance floor was packed with young, nubile bodies dressed in the latest brand-name clothes.

"You look amazing, Leena," Sunny said more than once.

"I told you, I told you," Suhani kept repeating as Leena blushed many shades of pink. Once he got her on the dance floor, Sunny refused to let her go, he put an arm around her and held her close. She was not totally surprised at her own reaction. She had been attracted to him since the first day she saw him at the temple. His warmth and laughter made her feel so comfortable. She laid her head on his chest and they danced together, oblivious to the world outside.

There was a lot of drinking, a lot of dancing, and even more drinking.

Suhani and Vinit spent the night dancing and then left to go home around two. Sunny offered to take Leena home later.

At around three in the morning they left the bar and headed to his home.

The sex was effortless, passionate, wild, quiet, remarkable, gentle, perhaps even good. She clung onto him wanting his strength to be hers, his smile, his attitude. She wanted a part of his spirit. "You are so beautiful," he whispered, "your gentleness ... your sweetness. I feel like I have been looking for you all my life."

The night was over in the blink of eye.

The next morning, she found herself telling him everything about the cancer, about her parents. They loved her so, gave her the perfect life and then were gone. He mostly listened, sometimes hugging her.

Sunny just let her cry, holding her closer as the tears flowed. She talked and talked and talked.

"You have to get this out of your system. Look at what it has done to you. It is holding you back. There is no way to go back but you can go forward. You have to let it go. You have to. There is no other way to live."

His logic was so simple. And yet, so hard for her to swallow. He was right. She knew it in her heart.

"Leena, you know I care for you a lot. But at this time in my life, I cannot promise you anything. I don't have a job, decent place to stay, nothing. I guess all I can promise you is a few special Sundays ... like this one."

With that, they left the warmth of the bed.

He dropped her back at Vinit's before heading out to finish the final illustrations for the novel that was almost done. He and Vinit were moving at lightning speed ever since they found a blog of a devadasi from Kerala. A blog of a devadasi! Leena was getting used to the enigma that was India. Sunny and Vinit were planning to leave Mumbai the next morning to travel to the backwaters of Kerala to meet this amazing devadasi who was blogging.

"How was last night?" Suhani asked the minute Vinit left the house.

"Oh, it was the best night of my life," Leena murmured and then burst into tears.

"What happened? Did he say something mean? What did he do? Why are you crying?" Suhani rushed over and hugged Leena.

"No, it isn't anything like that. I think, I think I have … he … he he told me last night that this was it for him and me … just a night … nothing more," Leena mumbled through her tears.

"Are you sure that is what he said? Sunny has a way of hiding behind words. Are you sure?" Suhani gently patted Leena's head but could not soothe the crying girl.

"I can't stay here anymore. I don't want this to go any further. I, I don't want this to go any further," Leena got up and rushed to the guest room and shut the door.

"She is in love with him, Mama, she is totally in love with him," Suhani heard Avni say. Avni had just come in from college and overheard the conversation.

The next morning, Leena flew back to her life in Washington, DC.

A Beautiful Boy

Mumbai, India

Dressed in a crisp white cotton *kurta pajama,* Sunny sat down on the cold beige marble temple floor and focused his gaze on the idols of the Gods in front of him. Dressed in blue silk and adorned with diamonds and gold, the statues looked majestic. He closed his eyes and began his annual ritual. Each year he would pray for the women in his life: his *hijra* mother, his socialite mentor, and now for the first time, his beautiful lost love Leena. It was always this way on his birthday, or what he guessed was his birthday. He spent the day at the local temple, thanking God for his own life but more for the people who saved him and let him live.

This birthday was different from all others. He had emailed Leena that morning, giving her the good news about his job back in Chandigarh. His proposal to use small neighborhood kids as spies to keep track of local pregnancies was accepted by the head of the clinic in Chandigarh. His boss had been thrilled at the idea. "This is great, the kids can come and tell us who in the house is pregnant so we know and then they can tell us when the baby comes." The local council, desperate to stop female infanticide, had approved the plan. Sunny was finally going back to being a doctor.

Leena had barely responded to any of his voicemails, emails, or text messages, and it bothered him.

Leena had left suddenly after he and Vinit went to find the blogging *devadasi*.

"I did not have the courage to tell her about my past. But she could have waited for me to at least come back. She left without saying goodbye," he told Vinit, who in turn reminded Sunny that this was at least the hundredth time he had said the same thing.

"This is the new world, *yaar*, call her, email her, tell her everything and then she will know why you behaved like such an ass that night and told her you could not give her anything," Vinit chided him.

"She won't respond to anything I send her. She barely sends a hello back. She hates me. I really blew it," Sunny had said, tears welling in his eyes.

The bells of the temple began to toll and the priest began reciting loud *mantras* in the background. The temple bustled with activity as seeking souls prayed for love, money, health, prosperity, revenge, babies, abortions, school grades, and job acceptance letters.

The louder the sounds became, the more quiet Sunny felt.

He began to breathe steadily and draw his thoughts closer and closer to his center. He closed his eyes. At first the images in his mind were fuzzy, but then as his spirit settled, he began to see a clear picture of Kamla Devi.

Shabbily dressed in a dark maroon sari, red bangles dangling on her arm and a name-calling foul mouth perpetually painted red by her incessant chewing of *paan* full of betel nuts, lime, a rose mix, and cardamom, rounded out with a stinking tobacco-filled *beedi* dangling from the left side of her mouth, Kamla Devi never mastered the graceful art of being a woman, but she always tried desperately to at least look like one. Her gold nose ring with a big red stone and her bright blue earrings never seemed right. Her hair never grew past her ears, and her teeth—the ones that were still in her mouth—showed years of tobacco and tea stains. Sunny missed her terribly.

He was thrown in her path during the Delhi riots of 1984, or so she told him. He was barely four years old. His memories of that day were her memories. Kamla, part of the Indian "invisibles," as a famous author once called them, was a *hijra*—not a true transsexual, she was a castrated man living as a woman. When she was first castrated, she lived with a group of other hijras who were either women born into men's bodies or naturally born with no distinguishable sex identity, making them instant outcasts of society. A small group of them lived in a shared house with a guru, a teacher, who guided them. She lived in that house for eighteen years before her guru let her move out on her own.

As a young boy of nine, Kamla had been taken away from his family and forcefully castrated. When she tried to go back but her father would not have anything to do with her. "What will people say? You are not a man anymore. You are not even a woman. There is no room for you in my house." So, resigned to her fate, Kamla had moved into the small group room that housed a tiny group of the local *hijras*.

The hijras earned their keep by singing and dancing at other people's happy occasions. Legend had it that these rejects of society possessed powers to grant any wish or hurl any curse. Some people hired them for their blessings, but most paid them off to prevent the *hijras* from cursing them. Kamla joined her hijra clan as they danced and celebrated the births and weddings at the homes of regular people; she celebrated the joys of the world as she wept at her own being.

Kamla secretly wished for many years that the kinder hijras would take her in. These were the true transgenders she had seen. They dressed like regular women and wore no garish makeup, they made an effort to fit into society, and even worked in offices. A few of them would even speak to her like, like, like she was human and not a weird specimen of spice. Instead, she was caught in an unusual, cruel, underground hijra community that stole kids and added them to their group. They took most of Kamla's earning each week, beating her if the numbers fell. She once tried to reach out to the other community and they welcomed her, teaching her how to dress and walk and talk. Then the elder of the group that abducted her found out. Kamla was brought back and beaten so badly that she was unconscious for three days. Now she no longer protested.

Kamla told Sunny that she first saw him when he was wandering the streets on that day from hell. A bomb had gone off in the heart of Delhi. The shopping area of Sarojini Nagar was totally destroyed. Different factions blamed each other for it and thirsty swords looked for revenge. Sunny, barely four, had been running blindly until he literally ran into her. He hid in her sari, tiny as he was. He barely moved when the armed man came up to them. *"Hindu ya Muslim?"* he yelled. *"HINDU YA MUSLIM?"* Kamla had shaken her head, *"Khud dekh le na*, see for yourself," she said as she clapped her big hands. She had no idea. The man pulled down Sunny's pants to look inside and had then turned and walked away. His penis saved his life. Later in life he would often joke that he was saved by the skin of his dick.

Kamla asked the little boy the names of his parents, his address, anything that would give Kamla a clue about where to take him. He was so stunned by the fire and chaos around him, she told him later, he could not even remember his own name.

"There was nothing left. Just bodies. No, that is not true. No bodies. Just pieces of people. Many of the *kuccha* homes were on fire. I tried to find your parents," she would tell him this story many times, almost as if to explain why she had bought him home with her.

Kamla named him Sundeep, the beautiful light of the sun, but neighbors began calling him Sunny and the name stuck. She added Suri as his surname a few years later while filing out a form for the local school. She knew no one by that name, but she knew it would give him some identity.

The first couple of days, he mostly followed her around the tiny hut quietly, holding on to the end of her sari like it was the jaws of life, never letting it go. He slept at her feet, ate at her side, and stayed within a few feet of her when awake. She hugged him once—he had smiled for the first time: a rare yet almost perfect smile. When the hijras from her clan came to collect part of her earnings at the end of the week, she hid him behind her cot and placed all the clothes she had on top so that they could not see him. The plan worked for that day.

When the children in the neighborhood called him to play cricket, he went out but mostly sat at the side and stared. A deathly blank stare that said volumes and yet no one ever heard. Occasionally he picked up the ball and threw it back at them. He just seemed to be there, not alive and not dead. Just there.

Then the local kids began to tell their parents about this radiant little boy, and the tongues began to wag. The gossips, from the local barber to the local washermen, all wanted to know, *Who is he? Where has he come from? Why is he with her?* People stopped him on the street to chat with him. Neighboring mothers brought bananas and a creamy almond halwa for him to eat, "*Kitna pyara baccha hai. Kis ka hai* Kamla? What a lovely boy, whose is it, Kamla?"

Kamla, conscious of her dark skin and skeleton-like body, constantly informed him that his looks would be his undoing. He never understood the logic. One day she explained: "People notice you, you are too fair. *Gora rang sau aab chupata hai* (fair skin hides a hundred faults). They want to look at you. They expect a beautiful boy to have a bright future. They want you in their life. Here, child, on the street, that is the curse of death. If you were plain, you would blend into the background. You would be like everyone else. But you are not."

She constantly told him to face down, to look at the ground as he walked and to not look people in the eyes. "Yours eyes are too bright, they shine and twinkle. There is laughter and allure in them. They will blind your future." He took it all to be the mutterings of an old soul and tried, at least when he was in front of her, to be the quiet, demure, subdued person she wanted him to be.

"You are very fortunate, God is on your side, you must have been born on a lucky night," she finally told him. She continued her rigorous efforts to look for his parents or some relative. No one knew where this child came from or where he belonged. She finally found the nerve to go and register his photograph at the local police *chowki*. She never heard a word back.

Most nights when they slept, she tied a small rope around his foot and held it in her hands. She would puff on her beedi and chew her paan, watching him until he was fast asleep. "I don't want people to steal you," she said. It took him years to learn that she was worried about child prostitution and his being abducted by the local gangs to beg on their behalf. She huddled close to him as he slept, terrified that the rats and cockroaches that lived with them would eat his tiny fingers and toes.

On nights when she could not sleep, she stared at him and wondered if she should take a knife and cut his face. Be cruel to be kind. Life is easier on the streets when you are ugly. She knew that. She had never been raped because no one would touch her. They said she was too ugly. No rape in this neighborhood was a miracle. But this child, on the brink of becoming a man, why had God been so cruel to him? Such perfect hair, such striking eyes, such a rare disarming smile. He looked like an angel. It would have served him better to look like the devil.

She enrolled him in a local school and later, as the years rolled by, he began to cheer up. The teachers, who themselves only had high school degrees, soon noticed his reading ability surpassed even theirs.

Their daily routine was simple but guarded. She cooked once a day in the evening, a bowl of rice and some lentils. That was dinner. Leftover rice was breakfast. After breakfast she accompanied him to the local tap in the middle of the neighborhood where they either filled a tiny jug with water or he took a quick bath. She then walked him to school. Later, she picked him up on her way back from work around lunchtime. Some days they stopped by the library on the south side of town. Well, technically it was a library. The air was musty, the furniture dusty, but Kamla took him there because no one looked at them, made fun of them, or asked questions. Many of the books had been destroyed because of a leaking roof. Sunny spent hours browsing torn, damaged books he could not yet read and looking through the rotting encyclopedias as if they hid the answers to all that ailed him.

After the library, she would feed him from a large leaf filled with lunch—some bread and a cooked vegetable. He was then allowed to play on the streets as long as she could watch what he was doing. He played marbles or cricket with the neighborhood kids but mostly he just watched.

One day an older child gave him an old carom board game—it consisted of a mostly rotten wooden board and some wooden coins. The goal of the game is to get the coins into the pockets at the four corners of the carom board using a striker, a small plastic disk—sort of like playing pool with coins instead of balls and a disk instead of a stick. His eyes lit up. It was the first time in his life someone had offered him a toy all his own. It became his solace. Although the game was supposed to have at least two players, he played by himself for hours on end. He cleaned a corner of the hut to place his carom board and would clean it each day. Kamla surprised him one day by bringing him a box of special borax powder to smooth out the surface of the game board. He was ecstatic and thanked her by filling the water jug by himself for the rest of the month.

Many evenings he helped her clean and cook and some days she even took him to the local market so they could indulge in his favorite snack, *gol gappas*—tiny fried balloon breads stuffed with potatoes and onions and then filled with spicy, minty water—all to be eaten in one bite.

Tuesdays were Kamla's holy days and he would accompany her to the local Hanuman Mandir so they could pray together. She taught him to fold his hands and close his eyes and chant *Jai Hanuman* in praise of the Monkey God.

As the priest chanted sermons and prayers, people would clap.

"Why is everyone clapping?" he once asked her.

"Our hands have a lot of poison stored in them, and clapping makes the poison go away."

"Why do they light incense sticks?"

"Every part of the prayer is meant to be good for everyone around the temple. The incense is used to make sure the air smells good for all of God's followers."

Her answers always sounded true, she was so convincing, but he was never sure.

At the end of the prayers, the priest always gave them *boondi*, tiny flour balls of sweetness soaked in clarified butter and a touch of cardamom. Sunny would cup his tiny hands together and accept the sweets. The priest would then add a red vermillion dot to his forehead and bless him. Kamla would be right behind him.

People always snickered and stared, but the kind old priest would stare them down or occasionally lecture them. "We are all God's children. Even them. Be afraid of His wrath if you look down on one of His own." It had no effect. They were constantly laughed at.

Once Kamla chased down one of the hecklers and beat him up with her bare hands until someone intervened.

"*Ek hijra aur ek chikna*" they said.[1]

"Yes, I am a hijra," she yelled, "so what is it to you?"

Generally people stared at him and then at her and shook their heads. "God knows where this hijra stole this child from? Poor thing. Is there no one who can help him? He will convert the boy to a hijra, too."

Sometimes the hecklers called Kamla a man. It was the only taunt that reduced Kamla to tears.

---

[1] Chikna is a slang term used to refer to a fair-skinned, good-looking man.

It made the strange relationship stronger.

The hijra and the chikna.

As Sunny grew older, lack of food became an issue. She constantly worried about his thin frame and not having enough to feed him. With barely enough to feed herself, she relied more and more on the kindness of others to feed him.

She devised a new way. Together they began to roam the religious sites in the city where people would throw money their way. He had seen other hijras make a scene and yell and scream, "Why are you throwing this money on the floor? I have hands, you can give it to me in my hands." But not Kamla. She would pick it up and continue walking.

People threw money to get rid of them. Some threw money and asked her to dance just so they could mock and laugh at her plight. Some thought she could tell fortunes and hung on to every word. "You will have many sons," Kamla would tell married women, "and your sons, they will care for you a great deal." The women would smile and pay her big money with dreams in their hearts.

She had another job that she never told him about, he found out years later. This one actually brought in some legitimate money. Money she had been depositing in a bank, just for him. After all, she said, she had no one else to give it to. The job she did was simple, humiliating but simple. She had been hired by local credit collection agencies. If someone defaulted on their bills, she was hired to go to their place of work and create a "hijra scene"—clap her hands loudly and dance obnoxiously till she embarrassed the person into paying his bills. It worked wonders: no one wanted this scene played out at their work place. The creditors got their money, and she was able to make a life. If that is what one would call this—a life.

And then one day it happened. Their worst nightmare came true. He was ten.

They came, a band of hijras, and took him away.

As he sat outside the house, squatting and using his fingers to wash out his mouth, a tall hijra dressed in a bright fuchsia sari came up from behind him and picked him up. No one stepped in to help. He never cried or struggled. His eyes never pleaded with her. He just curled up into a ball.

The young hijras walked over to Kamla to hold her back in case there was a struggle or she tried to stop them. "You knew this would happen," they said, echoing the thoughts in her heart. Tears ran down her cheeks; there was nothing that she could do. They had cared for her when she needed it; they had given her a place to belong. They had allowed her to work in their area. They felt she owed them.

And just like that he was gone. Gone.

She tried to find him over the next few days. Each day was torture; she would go from lane to lane, house to house, to all the hideouts she knew about, looking for any signs of her little boy. She even crept into the main hijra house to see if he was there. He wasn't, and the younger ones warned her to leave before the elders came in and found out she was meddling.

Then a strange thing happened. A few of the younger hijras stopped in at her tiny hut a few days later. "Do you know where he is? Is he here?" they asked. She found that odd. Why would she know where he was? She begged them to take her to him, to tell her what happened to him, but they did not. They threatened instead. "He has to stay with us. If he comes here you need to tell us. As soon as he shows up, don't delay." She was terrified; she had no idea why they were so angry. She had, after all, let them take him.

Even the neighborhood gossips did not know what happened to him.

That was a bad sign, she thought, usually they knew everything.

Two days went by. She wept each night for Hanuman to protect Sunny's soul. Then someone sent word.

The gossips had found something.

The eunuchs who took him tried to castrate him, without anesthetic as was custom. Instead they had got him drunk on some locally produced rum. They gave him many glasses of rum and forced him to drink until he first threw up and then passed out. The elders then readied themselves with the sharp knife, ready to cut away a part of him that was keeping him from joining their clan.

Kamla was amazed at how the gossips had found out about this secret custom. She knew in her heart that the gossips, for once in their life, were correct. Yet she did not want to believe them.

Squatting on the dirt floor of her tiny room, she began to weep for her son before the gossips finished their tale.

Her sobbing turned into a wail and she began to beat her chest, "Why, God, why that poor little boy. What will I tell him now? How will I tell him that he will never be a man or a woman?"

The gossips tried to calm her down, "Kamla, don't cry, wait, listen to the rest of the story."

She stopped for a minute.

"Just as they were beginning to recite the verses for the castration ceremony, one of the young hijras called out to them that the police had come. They all ran out of the house to stop *thullas* from coming inside."

Kamla's eyes widened. This was unheard of. They never left anyone during the ceremony, there must have been something else major that was happening.

"Sunny, where is he, what did they do to him, please, for God's sake, tell me, please?" she folded her hands in prayer and wept as she stared at them.

"When they came back, he was gone."

Gone? He was gone?

She began to laugh and cry, and cry and laugh. She could not believe his luck. God was kind to this boy. Getting away without being cut—this story would become a legend of sorts. Just then someone banged on her broken wooden door.

Loudly.

"Open this door, open up. Kamla, open the door, open it, fast, now." The banging got louder and louder and louder.

The priest placed his hand on Sunny's shoulder. "Sunny, *beta,* are you alright?" Sunny opened his eyes, transported from the memories of Kamla's tiny dingy dark room to this marvelously white and well-lit temple. "Who is Kamla? You were screaming her name with your eyes closed. Are you okay, my child?"

"Yes," Sunny could feel the tears running down his cheeks, "I am okay. I am so sorry to have caused a scene."

The priest smiled and walked away.

Sunny wiped his tears. He was sweating profusely. His mind wandered back to the day the hijras took him from Kamla. He had no memory of running away from the hijras. His last memory was one of waking up covered in a blue satin comforter in the home of a petite, fair, and very voluptuous Mrs. Karishma Mehra. She told him that she found him lying on the street and brought him home on instinct, much against the wishes of her lawyer husband, Ashish. His foot appeared to be broken and his arms had a few lacerations. Mrs. Mehra's words echoed Kamla's to Sunny's ears, "Such a good-looking boy, what were you doing on the streets? You look like you are from a good family. What were you doing out on the road in the middle of the night and is that alcohol I smelled on your breath? You were drinking, tell me?"

He had told Mrs. Mehra everything, as much as he could remember, anyway.

Instantly, she took on the role of a surrogate mother. He heard her fighting with her husband the second night he was there. "Who is this boy, Karishma? Why is he here? He cannot stay here. What if he is a crook? I don't care. You need to get him out of here." Sunny could barely hear her responses.

When he awoke the next morning there was no sign of Mr. Mehra.

Dressed in an olive green sari embroidered with brown and green flowers, and wearing beautiful freshwater pearl strings,

Mrs. Mehra was by his bedside with an old garrulous-looking physician.

"His leg will take at least two weeks to heal. It isn't broken … I think it is just a sprain. Don't let him walk or run around for now. The cast should help."

The doctor left and Mrs. Mehra gave Sunny some pills along with a glass of the freshest *mousambi* orange juice he had ever tasted. He could not take his eyes off her. He had never seen someone so ethereal in real life. She smelled of roses and her hands, painted with an intricate pattern of henna, as they touched his were softer than roses that he took to the temple.

It was only when she had left the room that he allowed his eyes to wander. He had never seen a room like this except in the Bollywood movies that Kamla would give him money to go see sometimes. Everything looked beautiful, pale blue silk drapes with hand-painted flowers, ornate and gilded lit wall sconces, a TV that seemed bigger than the size of his cot at Kamla's house, even the doors, the floor, did the rich have cleaner dirt?

Just as he was adjusting his eyes to the brilliance of the room, a young, wiry girl with dark hair came into the room holding a broom. "I am going to clean now. I am Madhu. Memsahib is so nice to bring you in, isn't she? She has a heart of gold." As Madhu swept the invisible dirt in the room, Sunny could barely keep his eyes open and drifted back to sleep.

He was awakened by a number of female voices. He opened his bleary eyes and saw six or seven well-dressed women staring at him. "See, Mrs. Sharma," Mrs. Mehra was saying, "see what I mean. He looks like he is from a good family. Ashish just does not see it. Well, now that he has gone to Calcutta for two weeks, I have two weeks to figure out what to do with this child."

All the other women seemed to synchronously nod in agreement as Sunny stared at their faces.

"So sad, *na*, I wonder where he came from" said one with a nose ring, "*Arre baba*, you have to be careful these days, so many little ones are thieves," said the one with garish red paint on her lips. "*Chalo, chalo*, now let's go out," and with that they were gone.

Madhu kept Sunny company in the days when Mr. Mehra was out of town and Mrs. Mehra was either out at her club playing cards or getting dressed to go out. About ten days into his stay, Mrs. Mehra had approached him about what he wanted to do.

"I want to go back to Kamla."

Kamla was ecstatic to see him. "I knew you would come back, I knew you would come and see me." The hugs and the tears flowed as a very self-conscious Mrs. Mehra waited at the doorstep.

Sunny introduced them and Kamla bent down to touch the feet of the young woman. "Thank you for taking care of my son, my beta."

Feeling awkward, Mrs. Mehra took two steps back.

"No, no, please don't worry. He is such a sweet boy."

Kamla glanced around her room, clearly panicking that she had nothing to offer the young woman as a reward, nothing but thanks.

"I will never leave you now, Kamla."

He remembered her expression to this day, it had become embedded in his mind. She very quietly said, "No."

The hijras would be back at any moment. The gossips who had been seated in the room had let themselves out as Sunny entered and Kamla knew it was a matter of hours before the hijras would return. Kamla bent down and touched the bandage on his foot again and again, as if willing it to heal.

It took them a mere twenty minutes to decide his fate.

Kamla handed him a bank passbook. Mrs. Mehra, in all her finery, was touched and volunteered to pay for his schooling at a boarding school just outside of Mumbai.

Kamla cried some more.

"Don't think I am doing this out of the goodness of my heart," said Mrs. Mehra, "I do nothing all day except spend my husband's money. He is never home. I figure when I die and God asks me what I did of value on this green earth, perhaps this one small thing will help me save face."

With that, Sunny left his eunuch mother to go with his new young socialite caretaker.

Kamla made him promise he would never write to her for fear that the hijras would read the notes and find him. She wrote him for a couple of years. The letters came from different cities around India. And then they simply stopped.

Mrs. Mehra never stayed in touch, either. She put him on a train to a school in Pune. When he arrived, a small suitcase in tow, an older gentleman who turned out to be the principal received him at the train station. His years there were spent in quiet learning. He kept to himself and no one seemed interested in his fascination with the carom board.

It was when he started medical college that Mrs. Mehra wrote him to say that she could no longer pay for his expenses. Her husband had now forbidden her from sending more checks.

Sunny, all of eighteen, found a way. One he never quite forgave himself for. He found out that bored, rich housewives paid top dollar to sleep with such a handsome man. He had a list of four lonely ladies, each of whom put him through one year of medical school. He provided company, often just listening to them talk about their busy husbands.

They all reminded him of Mrs. Mehra. She was barely twenty when he first met her, but she already looked like she had given up on life.

"I have nothing to do, no curtain call. Life has come and gone and I never even knew when I was supposed to be living and when I just started existing," she had told him.

For a few weeks he even had a real girlfriend. He had a t-shirt drawn up in her honor: KISS ME, I AM PUNJABI.

He graduated and went back to look for Kamla. The gossips, now old, told him she had died of dengue fever.

"You mean she still lived here? Her letters to me came from all over India," he said.

"She never moved. She would give a note to whoever was going out of town that month to mail to you. She wanted you to think she was away so you would not come back here and face the bad people." The gossips were delighted to share this big piece of news.

Sunny felt empty. He picked up his bag and took the next train to Punjab. He was going to work at the clinic in Chandigarh.

What was meant to be a dream job turned into a horror story when he found out about the abortions. He left Chandigarh in a heartbeat and now found solace in his small home in Mumbai.

He prayed for Kamla and Mrs. Mehra.

Today, for the first time, he prayed for Leena.

He opened his eyes and smiled as he thought of Leena. He leaned forward and lit a sandalwood incense stick for her as he had done for Kamla and Mrs. Mehra. The sweet scent of the sandalwood filled the air.

Leena made him smile; he had never encountered someone who carried the burden of the whole world on her shoulders quite so seriously. She was youthful, so precious, there was so much at her core. She had strength he envied. "I could never face cancer the way you have faced it, you are so brave," he repeatedly told her.

Vinit teased him, "Finally, you have fallen in love."

"No, no, she is just a friend," he protested at first, and then wondered if there was any truth to Vinit's statements. Could he fall in love with someone he could never be with? Her life was in America and his was in India.

"I was such an idiot to let her go, Vinit, do you think she will ever come back to me?"

"I don't know. Why don't you call her, man? You have been sulking since she left. What were you thinking anyway? Why would you let a girl like that get away?"

"I, I don't know. I ... you know my past. You know about how things went down during college. How can I tell her that? Tell her I was a prostitute? I don't even know who my parents are, where I come from, I know nothing. What can I offer her? I just wish I could get her back. I know she doesn't owe me anything but I thought she would call today."

She had sent a card that arrived a week earlier. It had a shimmering golden painting showing two people on a wooden boat with one simply holding a paddle and the other one actually maneuvering the boat. The note inside read, "Thanks for being my boatman, my *majhi*, and bringing me to shore. Happy Birthday!" He smiled at the note. She was wrong. He may have been her boatman, her guide, but he had not led her to shore. She had gone into the sea, into the open, alluring sea of life and adventure and of great tomorrows, leaving him behind on the shore of past loves, lives, and memories.

The vibrating of his cell phone brought him back to the present. Perhaps it was her.

The temple was loud and he could barely tell who was on the phone.

He got up and folded his hands in reverence and left the temple to go outside.

It was Vinit.

"Sunny, Leena's grandma just called. She is back in the hospital."

"Can you please call them back?" replied this most beautiful son of Mumbai. "Let them know I am on my way to DC."

Home Alone

Bethesda, Maryland
Late evening

Dolly stared at the decade-old pictures of her daughters, Neha and Amla, displayed in an ornate, gleaming, silver frame on the fireplace mantel. The gentle fire glowing in the fireplace warmed her as she stoked it. She picked up the frame and looked at the pictures—the girls had been a burden to raise— constantly demanding her time and attention. Why people had children was beyond her. But it certainly was such a gorgeous frame with leaves etched into it, she had purchased it at Tiffany and it was just perfect for the mantel. The red of her freshly manicured nails contrasted beautifully against the silver of the frame.

Dolly was glad the beautician came to her home twice a month to do her nails, wax her legs, clean up any stray hairs on her eyebrows, and of course give her a scalp massage. "You have to take care of yourself and look your best," she would tell her girls, who showed little or no interest in these feminine affairs.

For tonight, Dolly had chosen her outfit carefully—a baby blue sheer top embroidered with gold and silver petals that she wore along with fitted white pants. The ankles of her pants had blue, gold, and silver petals to match the shirt. She had let her long, waist-length black hair hang loose after washing it and drying it over sandalwood incense to make it smell just right. Just like the Bollywood star Rekha did in the movies. She ran her hand over the shirt to straighten it out—such a beautiful shirt and it fit her svelte figure so well, showing off the curves in just the right places.

Dolly placed the frame back on the mantel. Her girls, oh, she had given them so much and yet they were, well, just not good enough. No, no, not at all like her cousins' kids with gorgeous faces, fit bodies, and rich husbands. Perhaps that was too much to ask. At least Amla was beautiful, even though she needed constant attention. Neha was boring, with no interest in clothes, jewelry, or anything else for that matter—and heaven only knew where this child got such homely looks from. Two women who should have been a reflection of her, classy and beautiful, but sadly weren't.

It was past eleven and there was no sign of her *dear* husband, Shaya. Dolly checked her diamond-encrusted Cartier again. Shaya was supposed to have been home hours ago. She had called him at six and he said he was leaving the hospital; all he was concerned about was that child Neha had borne, what was her name? Ah, Myra. And what a silly name—Myra. And then he was going on and on about his sister-in-law. He cared only about them, not about her.

Dolly's own name had been a constant source of irritation for the longest time, a constant source of debate with her friends. "It is an Indian name: there are more Dollys, Pollys, and Rosies in India than you can ever count," she would tell them repeatedly. "But what is your real name?" they would ask, "your Indian name?" Finally, one day Dolly showed her friends her driver's license. "See, it is Dolly. Just Dolly, there is no hidden long, strange sounding name. It is really Indian." The questions still kept coming.

Shaya, where the hell was he?

Shaya. She repeated his name out loud. His name was also constantly debated. He was the typical American boy—blue eyes, blond hair, almost six feet tall with a dimpled smile—but his name? Shaya? No one had heard of it. She would laugh—here was a true Hebrew name but people still found a way to debate it.

One thing she had not counted on was how being a doctor would totally consume him. He never had time for her. It was all about the patients, as if those patients were going to take care of him when he fell ill or now as he was getting old. They came to him when they were sick, he took care of them, they got well, and then went their way. No one called to thank him. He did not seem bothered by it. It was an attitude she did not understand. What exactly did he gain from this useless profession?

She called Amla to see if her father was there. "Dad is not here, Mom. I talked to him earlier. He was worried about …," Amla tried to talk but Dolly cut her off.

"Don't bother telling me who he is worried about now. I am fed up with him, his patients, and that damn hospital," Dolly screamed into the phone.

"Mom, listen, I do want to talk to you about something," Amla tried to change the topic.

Dolly's heart ached for herself and some even for this child, Amla. Always needing attention and it was up to Dolly to provide it. This poor, ill child, it was almost as if God forgot to give her any immunity. Dolly listened for a moment and then gave her daughter every hint to remember it was her and Shaya's twenty-third wedding anniversary. Amla seemed clueless, consumed by the rash that had shown up on her hands.

Dolly hung up hurriedly and thought of calling Neha to see if she had heard from Shaya, but chose not to.

The last thing I need right now is to hear about that bastard grandchild. I did the right thing. There is no need for such a child in our house. How could my daughter have a child out of wedlock? Preposterous, she thought.

Neha had changed with the pregnancy, Dolly told Shaya. It was her damn liberal friends. They had no class and made her daughter the same. Neha walked around with that pregnant belly as if it were something to be proud of. The only relief was at least the baby was born pretty and fair-skinned. God alone knows who the father was. Dolly had tried to find out but Neha would say nothing.

"Who is the father, Neha? What is his family background? Does he have any money? I cannot believe you did this. I am your mother. You have to answer me. Aren't you ashamed? I raised you to be a moral person and now look at what you have done. At least the girl is fair."

Dolly threw Neha and the baby out of the house. She had a suspicion her husband was paying for the two of them but no proof yet. Neha needed to learn that sleeping around is for prostitutes, not for girls from good homes. Dolly just did not understand why this child could not have married someone decent. *Although with her looks anyone will do*, Dolly mused, *she won't get a prince, will she?*

Damn Shaya, she thought, *damn him*. Where was he? Did he not care that it was their anniversary? She had reminded him in the morning. Neither selfish daughter had remembered, either.

"In a way, both of them deserve the life they have, they had never learned to be like me," she often confided to her friends at lunch. The girls could have had it all and chose not to. Amla at least had a chance in life; Neha was a lost cause.

Dolly was happy with her life, minus her girls and that damn grandchild, very happy. She had all she needed from life, for the most part—a doctor husband, a sprawling mansion with a terraced backyard dotted with miniature ponds and fountains, maids to clean the house, a personal trainer who came to her home everyday, and ladies to lunch with. If the children had done anything to make her proud, that would have been the icing on the cake. But no, one had a bastard child and now dressed like a movie star wannabe and the other one, though so full of potential, was just not making an effort to meet the right man. No, no. She did not want to marry. Amla wanted to study. Study?! A waste of time and money.

Dolly left the living room and headed into the kitchen to make herself a cup of tea. She filled the gleaming stainless kettle with water and placed it on the stove. Her favorite tea had always been plain Japanese green tea, until she had discovered this treasure—the exquisite and expensive silver tips from Darjeeling—a rare tea made with hand-rolled tea buds. As the water came to a roaring boil, she switched off the stove and added the tea, gently stirring it to allow the leaves to release their sensual flavors. She selected her favorite tea cup, white bone china embossed with etchings of rose petals. She placed a strainer in the cup and poured in the tea from the kettle. The tea's amber hue showed best in this cup. She took a sip. Ah, the perfect cup of tea. Nothing helped soothe her nerves like this tea—no sugar or milk needed. She could no longer stand the taste of the commonplace green tea. She took the strainer over to the trash can to throw out the used tea leaves and saw the remnants of tonight's dinner in the trash.

Dolly had fully intended to cook a fabulous dinner of Shaya's favorite dishes: a gently simmered yogurt curry with spinach fritters and steamed rice. Truly, she had every intention of cooking dinner, but fate intervened—the stupid cops had messed up her schedule. Some police officers or detectives or whoever they were had shown up at the door asking all kinds of questions. She really did not care, she told them, all the better that *that* thing, that baby, was gone. The cops repeated their stupid questions again and again. At first she thought the police knew who had taken the baby. That made her very nervous. She had covered her tracks well. As their questions continued, it became evident that they were fishing for information. "I don't know who took her and I don't care, now please leave. You can ask Neha all the questions you like. To me this is like a blessing, we don't even know who the father is. This child is not part of my family," she had told them as firmly as she could.

After the cops left, she had decided to make Shaya the yogurt curry but there was no yogurt in the house and leaving to go to the grocery store meant she would miss *General Hospital*. Well, that was not entirely true. There was about a quarter cup of yogurt left but she needed that for her face mask in the morning. She tried to record *General Hospital* but the DVR would not cooperate. So she decided to skip cooking and order out instead. She laid the fried rice, chili beef, and kung pao chicken in beautiful serving dishes and had even lit a candle. That was hours and hours ago. When he didn't show up at nine, she ate. No point in wasting food. She placed his share in a Tupperware box and then in the fridge. At ten, she took it out of the fridge and threw it in the trash. The food was from his favorite Chinese restaurant. She had even called them twice to remind them to deliver it right at six-thirty when he was to come home, so that he could have a fresh meal. They did, but he did not bother showing up.

He did not deserve this thoughtful dinner.

She took her tea to the couch in the living room.

She had laid their wedding album out on the engraved and beautifully inlaid center table that she had found in Venice on a trip years ago. The tabletop flipped open, much like a music box, to play haunting tunes. Her parrot green couch was pristine in spite of being old. She cared for it well, making sure they did not spend time slumped on it. Anyway, it would soon be replaced with the custom couch she ordered last week in Paris.

The white lace on the cover of the wedding album had turned an aged cream and the edges had frayed, just like their marriage. She moved her fingers over the lettering—DOLLY WEDS SHAYA—and opened the page. The first picture ... was it really more than twenty years ago ...?

There she was, giggling, in all her gold and finery, as she frantically looked for something to dry her milk-soaked hennaed hands. It was a curious custom in her mind, for her and her groom to be asked to hold hands as her father drizzled milk and holy water on their hands. It signified their union but made her hands messy. Her oh-so-plain sister, sitting on her right, obliged with a clean handkerchief. Dolly marveled at the jewelry she wore—all custom-made pieces designed especially for her in Jaipur. Each diamond had been hand picked and set in gold. Her ring had a pink diamond, costing close to three-quarters of a million dollars; it was a gift from her father. Nothing less was acceptable. She knew he had taken a loan to do it but that is what fathers were for. The diamond was a bit small for her taste but nevertheless it was what she had asked for—a pink diamond mounted in a platinum ring. The gold band Shaya had given her paled a bit by comparison, but she did not mind. He had great earning potential and she knew he would get her bigger and better diamonds in time.

The magical night seemed endless as the priest's sermon continued in an ancient language, reserved for religious ceremonies, which neither Shaya nor Dolly understood. Shaya seemed mildly annoyed that no one bothered to translate it for him but Dolly had attended enough Indian weddings to know that the Sanskrit mantras held some sort of important meaning. "But really," she remembered thinking, "who cares?" This was about her getting married, not about some Sanskrit verses. No one thought this day would come for her; she had aged, they said. But she was beautiful, with dark curls bouncing around her shoulders, large black eyes, and a smooth, fair complexion, even fairer than the light-skinned girls the Indian community held in high regard. Yes, she was beautiful, men had a hard time resisting her charms. All through college, wedding proposals had poured in but she had no intention of marrying a chauvinistic Indian man who believed that women were meant to serve and to service men. That was not a life she wanted for herself. She wanted to marry an open-minded and wealthy American—someone who could take care of her and give her all she luxuries she so richly deserved.

So now there she was at twenty-five—an old maid by Indian standards—a blushing bride.

Dolly flipped over the pages of the album and remembered that when the ceremony had come to an end, the priest asked her and her groom to stand and bow to the elders. Her childhood friends had whispered in her ear of naughty things that would follow that night. They would die if they knew she was two months pregnant! Against her parent's wishes, she had gone to the US to visit friends. She met Shaya at a friend's party and fell in love instantly. She knew he was captivated by her beauty; he did not stand a chance of resisting. Within two months of their meeting, she was pregnant. And now here they were getting married.

The next photo showed her mother draping her with a warm shawl to ward off the mild chill. Delhi in October was still warm and so she had shrugged the shawl off, wanting to show her bridal sari. Relatives and friends congratulated her. She stared intently at the photos: she was glowing while Shaya appeared to be scowling. This was her day and he had tried to ruin it.

Dolly turned another page of the album. Even now, this one picture brought tears to her eyes—her sister approaching her with a clear plastic bag of puffed rice as her brother stood on the side. She remembered it as if it had happened only a few hours ago: it was that moment of leaving her family. The rice meant she was getting ready to leave her father's house forever. The sequence of events that happened next was deeply ingrained in her mind—her brother approached her slowly, as if buying time: the longer he took to walk, the longer she would stay with them. He then took her by the arm and moved her toward a waiting car. Her sister handed her the rice. With each step, she scooped handfuls of puffed rice and threw them over her head. Each scoop meant that she was leaving her "good deeds" behind as blessings for her family. They would reap the benefits of her goodness. The tears came rushing. Each scoopful she dedicated to someone—her mother, her sister, her brother—and then she stopped in her tracks. This one was for her father. She turned to him, held up her folded hands and with her eyes said goodbye. It was truly a made for Bollywood moment. Such perfection.

The pictures of her brother reminded her of her glorious childhood. Each year she had tied a *raakhi* around his wrist in keeping with tradition. Each year the raakhi was different, showcasing whatever was "in style" in the market. From simple threads to overly jazzy threads adorned with plastic sunflowers, he adored them all! Their mother explained that his sisters tied the thread to show their love for him. In return, she told him, he was to be their protector and promise to be their strength. He used to laugh at this old-fashioned custom. "A strong woman like Dolly doesn't need me," he joked. He had no money then and borrowed cash from his dad to buy her customary gifts. The memories brought a smile through the tears. She loved her brother and missed him dearly. Her sister had been jealous of her looks and they had never really got along.

At the wedding, her brother had been her savior and it was he who helped during the final goodbye. "She is all yours now," he told Shaya in the car, "hair salon bills, tone deaf singing, and all."

Then he turned to her. "*Di*, how much gold are you wearing—Dad must be broke now."

And again to Shaya, "Do you know about her midnight munchies habit? You will need to keep a close eye on your refrigerator."

That was the last time she saw her brother. He flew early the next morning for a meeting in Mumbai and was still there when she left to go back to the US with Shaya.

A week after her wedding, the hellish news arrived. Her dear, loving brother who put her needs ahead of his, who was always around for her, had been in a grisly accident. He had driven his motorcycle straight into a truck and was not wearing a helmet at the time of the crash.

Dolly never went to back to India to say her final goodbye. She firmly believed that as long as she did not go there and see her home without him, he would live forever and give her strength as he had done at the wedding. She did talk with her father about how the property would be divided now that he was gone and was assured that now it would be divided equally between the two girls. "Good, that is what he would have wanted," she responded.

The last few pictures in the album were taken in front of the hotel where Shaya was staying. He had no parents and his brother, Jake, had refused to come to the wedding, so Shaya had come alone.

Dolly and Shaya—married.

The baby would be born to them as a couple, as it should be, and not to her as a single mother.

They flew back to Maryland after the wedding. Shaya seemed distant and sulked. She wondered if he felt trapped. They had argued endlessly about her having an abortion after they returned from India since early testing, the nuchal test, had showed serious abnormalities with the baby.

"That is just your way of taking this baby away from me so that you can divorce me. That is why you are saying all this. How can this test be right? I am barely twelve weeks pregnant, it is too early," she complained bitterly to him. "I don't believe in all these tests. I don't know how I let you talk me into them. I am not that old. This baby will be fine, Shaya. Why don't you want this baby? As a doctor you think you know everything. Well, the tests are wrong. There is going to be nothing wrong with this baby."

"You are being unreasonable, Dolly, this baby has serious problems—it could have multiple heart defects or Turner syndrome or worse. I promise you that we will have more children and I am *not* doing this to divorce you. Please listen to me," he had tried to reason with her.

After her brother's sudden death, her argument changed.

"No, no, I know this is my brother coming back. We call this reincarnation back home. He is coming back to me in the form of this baby. It happens all the time … I can tell you about ten Bollywood movies where this has happened and they don't lie about such things," she retorted.

Unfortunately, the tests had been right. Her first baby, before Neha and Amla, before these girls, her first-born, a son, born a few months after her brother's death, had been stillborn. The fetus had a serious form of cystic hygroma, almost always fatal in babies.

Shaya had not allowed her to name the baby. It was too much for her to take—her brother's death and then the baby. When the baby was stillborn, something inside her head snapped. Deep in her heart, she knew this was not her fault. She had been so good about taking care of her health. She had eaten well, was taking her vitamins. She suspected it was Shaya's genes that contributed to the issue. It had to be. She had done nothing to deserve this.

Regardless, now her brother would never come back to take care of her. His spirit would be lost forever in time and it was all Shaya's fault. He was a doctor. Surely, there was something he could have done. No, he just wanted her to end the pregnancy. The constant argument on the topic became a source of an intensifying rift between the couple.

Shaya started to become strangely distant after his son's untimely death. She tried to get him to pay attention to her and take care of her. She had needs, too. At least he continued to work and gave her a healthy bank balance so she could survive.

He did soften, a few years later, when Amla and Neha were born. It was the only time she saw him let his guard down and really relax—with his girls. He loved them and they doted on their father. It seemed to distance him more and more from her. She hated that the girls did that. He gave them all his attention, even what should have been reserved for her.

Dolly got up to make herself some more tea. It was past two in the morning and he was still not home. She kept vigil staring outside her window. It looked cold out there. It was terrible being alone on your anniversary night.

As she turned away from the window, she heard the garage door opening. She ran toward it. He was home and she could not wait to see what present he had got her. It was such a special night.

He stepped out of the car looking harried. His eyes were swollen; it looked as though he had been crying. Before she could ask … "It has been a horrid night," he whispered. "It's Jeanine, she was in the ER all night. She may not make it. He is a mess, Jake … he is just a mess. He was up all night weeping … And the police came by, Myra is still missing …"

"But it is our anniversary," she began to say. Then she stopped. "I am sorry about the, the ... the baby," she said gently, barely acknowledging the news about her missing grandchild. Then she added, "You must be so upset. I know you wish that were me. So that you would be free of me, instead of Jake becoming free of his wife. So you could be free for life."

"I can't believe you said that, Dolly. It is not all about you, all the time," he said incredulously. "She may die and all you can think of is you? I was at the ER all night. She may die, you hear me, *die*. And our grandchild is out there somewhere.... the cops cannot find her. Doesn't that bother you?"

Dolly was fuming, her face turned bright red and she placed her hands on her waist and stared at him. Clearly he had forgotten their anniversary and was focused on strangers. Pathetic. He had a wife at home and his attention should have been on her, especially tonight.

The bastard child and someone else's wife, how typical, she thought. Damn Jeanine and Jake. They were his true family, not her. They had never warmed up to her or her to them and still Shaya was so concerned about them versus her.

Had Shaya even called poor Amla back? She had been frantic about her symptoms. "Did you even call Amla, she says her rash is back?" she asked. He looked at her incredulously, "Dolly, that child is a hypochondriac. There is nothing wrong with her. She tends to develop these rashes when she is under stress. How many times have I told you that? Don't encourage her. There is nothing wrong with her."

"That is what you say so you don't have to care for us," she screamed. "You are too busy wallowing in someone else's sorrow to look after your own wife and daughter."

She left the garage and stormed back into the house.

Shaya slammed the door to the car. As much as he had loved and cared for her for so many years, some days he simply hated her. Her self-absorption never ceased to amaze him; just when he thought it could get no worse, she would outdo herself. Like tonight.

As he stepped into the house, he found himself reminiscing. This house used to be filled with glorious scents and smells. Tempering garlic and simmering curries, but it seemed like that was decades ago. Now it smelled hollow, if hollow has a smell. Actually, it does—it smells like sandalwood incense and arrogance. He caught himself walking gently, not wanting to step on his broken dreams that were scattered in every inch of the house.

He married someone he thought was a feisty, beautiful young woman with big dreams and tinkling laughter that was contagious. He lived now with a bitter, cynical, and somewhat paranoid silhouette of that woman.

He understood her pain after her brother and then their son died. But the girls had bought such joy to the house. For a few years after their birth, she had even seemed happy. They hired a full-time nanny to help with the girls. Dolly seemed delighted and played with them, took them out and even cooked, even made his favorite meals. But slowly her attitude began to change back to the time of the deaths. As the girls demanded more attention, she began to sulk. She began to resent being the caregiver, even with a full-time nanny, and constantly complained about her freedom being taken away from her. She used every excuse she could find to leave the house—sometimes for days on end, traveling around the world with one of her socialite friends. Homemade meals, family time, and spirituality were not part of their family vocabulary.

He sat down on the couch. They had bought it years ago so they could snuggle and watch movies together. It still looked like it had just come from the store, unused. And now there was a new couch coming. Sometimes he wondered when she would replace him. He was the only thing original to the house.

His thoughts drifted to Jeanine. What good was his medicine when he could not save family? How in the hell did she get meningitis? He knew it was a matter of hours before it killed her unless there was a miracle. He wanted to stay at the hospital, but Jake had sent him home. "Dolly is waiting for you. Besides, you have done all that you can here. Go home and rest, I will call you if there is any change in her."

Shaya knew he should have excused himself from the ER when they wheeled her in, but he could not. He cared deeply for his brother. He began to weep. He envied their life together. They seemed so in love. What would happen to his brother if his lifeline, his wife, did indeed die?

He heard Dolly banging the doors of the bedroom and tried to ignore her.

Their meeting had been a mere coincidence. He had just finished med school and started his residency. It was his first night off from a grueling schedule at George Washington University Hospital where he was doing the pediatric rotation. His friend Gordon had called and insisted he come over for a drink with a few friends. A few friends turned out to be about fifty people. Tired and bored, Shaya stood on the deck of his friend's home and sipped his Diet Coke. The thirty-hour round-the-clock residency had been more exhausting than he cared to admit. As he yawned and decided to leave, a young Indian woman came up to him and introduced herself. A backless, flowing purple dress showed off her flawless back. She smiled, "I am Dolly," and offered him her hand. He noticed her rings, five of them, all oxidized silver, glittering even in the dark. "I don't know too many people here. I am just visiting from India." They began to talk and he was completed awed by her confidence and attitude. She seemed to know exactly what she wanted and how to get it. He noticed it in many of the young Indian residents he worked with at the hospital. It seemed to be an inbred quality in Indians—a passionate pursuit of whatever it is they desired. *In hindsight,* he thought, *I should have realized that what she desired most was money or a man with money.* But back then, an exotic beauty with gorgeous eyes with a dress so deep in the back that it showed off her thong caused a tired young resident to rethink his idea of a fun night. They left together and she moved in within a week. She wrote her parents to say she was not coming back just yet.

Within two months, she was pregnant.

Shaya remembered how she announced the news. He had come home late at night to find her at the table with an unusual dinner prepared—baby carrots, baby peas, baby zucchini. He ate it all without noticing. "Did you notice something different about the food?" she had asked. "Nope. Why? Let me tell you about what happened today …" he had said, wanting to tell her about his new assignment. She would hear nothing of it. "I am pregnant and we need to get married." Pregnant? Married? The news hit him hard. He barely knew her and what he had begun to know, he did not like. She was great as a date and for some fun, but Shaya did not want to spend the rest of his life with her. He tried to tell her gently that it would not work. She left the dining room and locked herself in the bathroom.

Five minutes later, she screamed. He ran and banged on the door for a full five minutes before she opened it. She had used a razor to attempt to slit her wrists, a tiny trickle of blood flowed from the wrist—she held her hands under running water so the blood would not clot and she could bleed to death.

She began cursing him, "I will kill myself before I go home shamed like this!" Instantly, he felt like a selfish son of a bitch. Here was this poor young woman, pregnant by him and he was telling her he could not marry her. He hugged her and then bandaged her wrist. "Don't worry, it will be okay."

It never was.

His own private hell began from that day.

His eyes caught the wedding album on the table. Their wedding day—it was one of the saddest days of his life. He knew no one at the wedding. Neither his brother nor his sister-in-law attended the wedding. He had never felt so alone in his life. There were literally a thousand people at the wedding and he knew only Dolly. She was so engrossed in the wedding that she barely acknowledged him, much less took the time to introduce him to someone, anyone.

He hated every minute of the wedding, every single thing about being with her family.

All his life, all he had ever wanted was a family. When he was about eight years old, his father and mother died in a car accident. His brother was eighteen and just starting college. His parents left a small amount of money for them and, in the wake of their deaths, their life insurance policies provided a cushion for his brother's and his education. His brother cared for him alone for a year or so and then married young. His sister-in-law, Jeanine, turned out to be a blessing; he had been scared that she would hate having a ten-year-old in the house. But she was a middle school teacher, very religious, and loved him from the first time she set eyes on him. They raised him— through high school and girlfriends, soccer games and tennis matches, piano lessons and medical school. Jake gave him the biggest surprise for his sixteenth birthday and took him to New England to watch the Patriots play. It was special in more than one way—the Army drafted Jake for a few years around the same time. Jeanine still took care of Shaya during the two long years. In more ways than one, he felt more like a son rather than Jake's sibling. "It will never work," most people had warned them, but it did. They stayed together and enjoyed life as a family until Shaya met Dolly.

Jake and Jeanine took an instant dislike to her, often referring to her as an "Asian gold digger."

"She is so fake, Shaya, don't you see it?" Jake tried to gently advise his much younger and gentler brother.

"She only wants to marry you for the money you will make. Do you even know if this baby she is carrying is yours?" Jeanine added.

Shaya fought his brother tooth and nail. "She is a good person, a bit high-strung but she is good. I know it will work out. I am sure the baby is mine, why would she lie to me?"

Then he agreed to marry her and on her insistence went to India for the wedding. Jake refused to go with him. "I cannot watch you destroy your life. I will be here when you get back, but Shaya, please, please reconsider. You barely know her and what we have seen of her—she is just not for you." Jake's pleas fell on the deaf ears of a responsible but naïve young man.

India took Shaya by surprise. He had never left the shores of the US and India was a totally new world for him. Her family was larger than life. Uncles, aunts, cousins swelled in numbers by the minute. They all smiled at him, said hello, and then talked around him. They spoke in Hinglish, a strange mix of Hindi and English, and he could not follow it. They seemed to be all entwined in a single soul, all headed to the same goal—the big wedding. And a big wedding it was—her father informed him that they were expecting close to a thousand people. He tried to make an effort to talk to her older relatives and her parents but their responses alienated him further.

"Shaya, what type of name? Ah, Jewish? India has Jews, too—we are the only country not to persecute your kind," one said.

"What will you wear for the wedding? You must wear Indian clothes. Yes, like your Indian dress today, you look so nice, so Indian," another said, touching Shaya's Indian outfit that Dolly had insisted he wear when meeting her relatives.

"How can I look Indian? I have blond hair," he whispered, but no one was listening.

"Oh poor boy, he has no parents. No friends? No one came with you for the wedding? Why your brother did not come? Why? He does not like us?" Comments like these pricked his easygoing manner.

Although he considered himself to be quite cosmopolitan, he found that he could not connect even with her siblings or her younger, well-educated cousins. They seemed to live in a different reality—endless shopping trips, servants at their beck and call, an unending obsession with food ... He tried to make small talk but to no avail.

The ceremony, he remembered, in itself was beautiful, his bride glowing. It did annoy him that the entire ceremony was being conducted in a language that neither Dolly nor he understood, but everyone seemed to be okay with it. Shaya had prepared his own vows. He asked to read them and Dolly's parents politely informed him that, "It is not our way, son. You will have to listen to what the priest says." He so wanted to tell her he loved her, but she was so taken with the idea of getting married that she seemed to have forgotten he was real and there, and that she needed to be there with him.

Finally, his patience ran out when all the crying started. After the ceremony was completed, all six hours of it, her mother began to cry and then her father and then her sister and then her cousins. They were all wailing as if he was the sinister evil kidnapper who was whisking her away. People cried at Jewish weddings and American weddings but mostly quietly. The scene unfolding before his eyes was more that of mourning at a funeral than a celebration of two souls coming together in a wedding.

The worst of it all was his new wife's behavior. She treated him as if he were a mere superfluous addition to the day. He tried to talk to her. "Dolly, can we talk? I want to connect with your family. It isn't happening." She was oblivious and had the same response each time, "Don't worry, this is how things are here."

He wanted to be a part of the celebration, instead he felt like an outsider standing and watching as his brother's words—*she doesn't really love you, she only loves herself*—became a reality.

When the news of her brother's death came, Dolly began to change. She began reading every book she could find on reincarnation and convinced herself that her brother was coming back in the baby's body. She began to obsess about what she ate, what she drank, and even who she talked to because the baby, her brother, was listening.

When the baby died, they had both been devastated. She kept insisting that he had killed the baby and could not save him. He was a doctor, how could this happen to them, she kept saying. He felt his love, his understanding, and his ties to his wife died that day with the baby.

Jake often asked him why he didn't just get a divorce. "Come on, bro, we're Jewish," Shaya joked, "suffering is our birthright." Her tantrums, her demands, and her demeanor got more outrageous with age. She wanted to go on cruises and buy luxury apartments in Paris; she wanted more diamonds and then a Bentley. "I cannot afford these things," Shaya told her. "What do you mean? You are a successful doctor with a great practice, why can you not afford this? You promised you would get me all I wanted and take care of me, now you are letting me down. When I go to Paris, I want my own apartment." He rented her a place at $4,000 a month.

"My wife has what I call PDS," he confided to Jake one day.

"What is that? Is it a medical term?"

"No," he laughed, "I call it the perpetual disappointment syndrome. She is perpetually disappointed in everything I do." He failed to mention the verbal abuse that came with Dolly's continuous piercing comments.

He missed seeing his brother more regularly. Before Dolly came along, they were inseparable—sharing a room, cheap food, and bad life advice. Dolly's entry into Shaya's life, particularly after the wedding, had strained his relationship with Jeanine and Jake. Family get-togethers were more of a pain than pleasure. So now Shaya would stop into Jake's office whenever he could. They would share espresso and laughs over old memories, like the time Jake was so drunk in college that he peed into the mailbox, or the time that Shaya asked a girl out at a bar only to realize later that it was a drag queen. Shaya still laughed at their ONG quip which was inevitably shared each time they met. They both shared a deep love for fried foods and often teased each about being the ONG crowd—Eat Oil and Produce Natural Gas.

"Why do you stay with her, Shaya?" Jake asked him that every chance he got. And it had been twenty years.

At first he stayed with her for his girls. Any mention of divorce and he knew she would have kept the girls from him. Then they were older and went away. Now it was a question of company. "Leave her and go where?" What he hated more than staying with her was the thought of being alone. At least there was someone in the house when he came home.

He walked into the kitchen and decided to make himself a sandwich. It had been over thirty-six hours since he had eaten. There was no bread so he took out a few slices of cheese and a fruit cup. He peeled open the plastic wrap from the cheese and headed to the trash can. When he opened the can, he saw the remnants of their anniversary dinner. Take-out Chinese, how thoughtful. He threw the cheese in with the wrapper and left the fruit sitting on the table.

He grabbed his phone from his pocket hoping there was an email, text, or some message from Neha about Myra. Nothing. No news on the baby.

He went back out to the garage and opened the door of the passenger side. The tiny Tiffany-blue bag sat on the passenger seat. He pulled out the small box inside and opened it: two-carat diamond earrings. Just what she had requested.

He came back into the house and placed the jewelry box on top of the album, turned the lights off and went to the couch to lie down. His head was pounding as all the anxieties of the day seemed to melt into a sharp dagger that someone kept stabbing him with, right between the eyes.

His cell phone rang. It was Jake. Jeanine had opened her eyes.

Best Friends

Alexandria, Virginia

Tony stood outside Mina's bedroom door as she screamed. Raw, bone-chilling screams like an animal writhing in pain. Gut wrenching enough to make you want to throw up. The demons had slipped into her blood a year ago. The devil's sugar had changed her forever.

Years later, even in the quiet of the day, those screeching, painful yells for mercy, sometimes begging for death, those screams would haunt him. Their excruciating echoes piercing his ears.

But today, he did not know that. Today, he had to help her. He had to let her scream and yell and cry. It had been a week of disaster on top of disaster. Mina's grandmother Emmani, who had been her sole caregiver, had died earlier in the week. Mina had reacted, or in his opinion totally overreacted, to the death of a very sick ninety-year-old by going on a drinking binge and then the drugs again. Now, they had just returned from the police station. A police officer had taken her in after seeing her slumped on the side of the road. She just sat in one corner staring at him as he tried to talk to her. "Miss, do you remember me? This is the fourth time I am bringing you in here. Do you hear me? If you want to drink, I cannot stop you, you are old enough. But you cannot be out on the streets. It is so dangerous. Miss, are you listening?" The police officer may as well have been talking to the wall.

Mina had called Tony to come get her and just as always, he sprinted to her rescue.

"Take care of her. She has been through so much," the old police officer told Tony. Tony nodded. This had become a routine of sorts.

Once they were out of the station, Mina became hysterical, incoherent, and her paranoia came forward in full swing.

"I let you down again, Tony. The cops think I will tell them? They are fucking morons. How can I do it? Those guys will kill me if I rat on them. What the fuck are they thinking, Tony. I am so fucking tired. My brain is fried." Her rant continued for an hour interrupted only by bouts of vomit until there was nothing left in her system.

Tony said nothing; it really did not matter if he said anything. She was not in a state where she could comprehend any kind of logic.

The old police officer had tried to help her when she began throwing up at the station. She yelled so loud that she almost lost her voice, "FUCK YOU. FUCK YOU. FUCK YOU." Tony showed up just in time and dragged her out of there. "I am so sorry for the way she is. I will take her," he told the old cop.

Finally, at home, after bouts of yelling and vomiting, Mina finally collapsed on the couch.

He sat across from her and watched her waste away. If he tried to hold her, she would punch and push him away; if he sat away from her, she would accuse him of not caring. Unsure of what to do, he just watched her for signs, hints on how he should behave with her.

"I have to get this shit out of my system. Can you help me? Please, help me? I want to go cold turkey. I don't want any fucking rehab. I just want to do this on my own. Will you help me? Come on. Say something, damn it. Will you help me? Don't you think I can do this? I can do this, right? I have to get this crap out of my system," she begged him.

Tony simply stared at her, once again unsure of what to do; cold turkey was not something he thought she could handle, not in this state of mind anyway. His calves hurt, his back hurt, and muscles he never thought existed hurt; he was exhausted from riding his bike, just having returned from a two-week biking tour of the Northeast.

"Yes, I will do this with you, but Mina, this is a crazy idea. Why not try the rehab? They will know how to handle it. I won't know what to do."

The devastated look on her face guilted him into agreeing.

"Okay, fine. I will be with you, but if it gets really bad, I am calling 911."

Reluctantly she agreed. Around midnight, she decided she was ready to go it alone.

"Are you sure, Mina?" He tried to steady his trembling voice.

"Yes."

She got up and left to go into the bedroom. She smiled at him and then shut the bedroom door; it was going to be a long night.

Letting go the drugs, the drinking, would be hard, he knew.

It meant she had to face up to who she was, face all the realities she had been avoiding.

"Leave the drugs, they don't make you happy," Tony often told her.

"Why the fuck does everyone always want to be happy? What is it about happiness? Why do people not ask for good health or a shitload of money? At least that would last a lifetime. Happiness is a fucking joke," was her trademark response.

The day after her mother died, she decided happiness was not for her.

"I don't want happiness. But, just once in my life," she once told Tony, "just once, I want everything to be still, to be quiet. I want to hear my heart beating. I want the thoughts to stop. I want my mind to be quiet. Is it possible to stop thinking? To just be?"

Now, inside her room, she sat on top of the faded blue comforter with a sunflower print. She sat and stared at the casually framed picture on the wall. Her mother Jaya's kind face looked down upon her. It was taken years ago in the local mall. It was her favorite picture of the two of them together. Mina was about five and sat on her mother's lap, both of them dressed in their favorite pink outfits, matching, of course.

"I was already forty when you were born, but you so wanted a brother," her mother often reminded her of the day that photograph was taken. "You asked the photographer if he could help your mommy have another baby! Your words, I still remember them, 'I want a little brother. Can you tell my mommy how to have another baby? Can you show her so that I can get a brother?'" They laughed about it each time.

Mina and Jaya lived in an insulated world of material luxury. Although Jaya spent long hours at NASA and worked almost every weekend, Mina could not recall a day when her mother had not spent time with her. Jaya helped with homework, class projects, and even occasionally took days off to volunteer at Mina's school. Each night before going to bed, they played either card games or board games. And they talked, a lot. Jaya was spirited, well-traveled, and had a story for every topic under the sun. "When you turn seventeen we are going to take a year off, before you head off to college, and do this," Jaya said one day pointing to a book, *1001 Places To See Before You Die*.

"I don't think we can hit all of them but I will let you pick your top one hundred and we will see the world together, Mina. You will love it, there is so much out there to do and see, I figured I would give you a head start!" Quickly, it had become Mina's favorite book and she loved to lose herself in its pages and imagine what it would be like to visit each one of them with her mother. She wrote and rewrote her list of places she wanted to see: the balloon safari over Masai Mara, sailing the Grenadines, the Pushkar Camel Fair, the backwaters of Kerala, the Buddhas of Borobudur, and more. The list changed each month as she spent hours at the library researching each place and making to-do lists of what she and Jaya could do in each place, where they could eat, where they could stay, and even the kinds of clothes and shoes they could buy from each place.

Mina sometimes quizzed her mother about her dad.

"Who is he, Mom? Why won't you tell me?"

Her mother's response was always vague and inconsistent.

At first, Jaya told her that her father was a young Army man. Then, the story changed and he was a Marine. A few months later, he was an Army man again. There were no wedding pictures or any other pictures of her father that she could find.

Mina confronted her mother, "So, which one is it? Or did he work for the Navy, Army, and Marines at the same time? Or was he a super-secret FBI agent and that is why you cannot tell me who he is?" When her taunts, sarcasm, and even threats to run away yielded no response, finally Mina gave up asking. It was on her thirteenth birthday that Mina finally learned the secret and the true meaning of the adage, "be careful what you ask for."

Mina was in the attic of their small Bethesda home trying to find her thirteenth birthday present. Jaya had promised her a computer. She could not wait to get her hands on it. She was sure her mother had hidden it, as she liked to do with all gifts. She searched through all the shelves and old suitcases but could not find a box large enough (or new enough) to be a new Dell desktop. While searching, she came across a box of old papers, and began to leaf through them. Most of them were certificates showing off her mother's degrees that contributed to the alphabet soup after her mother's name. Jaya had dual masters and a doctorate, and worked as a scientist at NASA. Mina kept reading through the papers, marveling at her mother's various achievements and successes in the professional world. From college degrees to professional accreditation, from local awards to dinners at the White House with the main man himself, her mother was truly a professional success.

All these papers but no gift box! Mina was just about to give up when she stumbled on a rather large brown box. It was plain, old, and decrepit looking. She picked it up and turned it and shook it, nope, no sound. There were a few spiderwebs on it; she cleared them and then brought the box to her nose and smelled it. Nope, no smell, no sound, and it wasn't much to look at either. Bored with her find, she was about to place it back in the suitcase where she had found it when it slipped out of her hands and spilt its frayed contents onto the floor.

Mina stared at the old papers and folders. Damn it, now she would have to clear this before Jaya found her and got mad for "making a mess of my papers." A white piece of paper with Jaya's handwriting:

Nature whispers its precious riches into my belly
I try to hold them inside
But they leave
Why don't they want to be mine?
Perhaps to escape, to be free
The fault is mine

A womb weak, damaged
It cannot hold onto the tiny souls
Perhaps people are right:
The children of barren women belong in a better world,
In nature's own playground in the sky

"Mom used to write some strange poetry," she thought to herself.

She began picking up the papers hurriedly at first, then stopped when she read the title of the red folder, "CJ Sperm Bank—List of donors." What the hell was her mother doing with a list of sperm donors? She began to read the file.

Her mother's handwriting was all over the list with comments on each donor and then there it was, circled with a pencil: "Thirty-year-old male, Ivy League graduate, plays the piano, enjoys traveling, near-genius IQ, surgeon at major hospital." The forms went on to describe physical characteristics, family medical history, detailed illness descriptions, even when the man lost his virginity, how much he drank a week, what his favorite vegetables were, what types of girls he liked, what he did for fun, everything you ever wanted to know about a stranger but were afraid to ask. Another red folder contained information on egg donation. It contained similar information on egg donors. The formatting of the documents indicated that they came from two different clinics.

A sperm donor? An egg donor? What was her mother doing with this information? Mina did not have to search too much longer to find out. A light blue folder had a letter from a fertility clinic confirming an appointment for an IVF procedure to begin. It also listed donor numbers and names of the clinics from where the specimens would be obtained. Mina glanced at the date on the letter. It was dated eleven months before the time of her birth.

So her mother had used an embryo made from two virtual strangers who had presumably never met each other to get pregnant? Why had she not found a partner? Why had she not even bothered to use her own eggs?

Does this make me a bastard child? An orphan? An adopted child?

Mina sat down with the papers in her lap. *Who am I? What am I? What do you call the children of barren women other than pathetic? Why did Mom never tell me? OH MY GOD—she is not my mother. She probably does not even know my real father or my real mother. Who am I?*

It bothered her that her beautiful mother could not find anyone to start a family with and resorted to this kind of nonsense. Was she really the result of a man loving a *Penthouse* page in the doctor's office?

Her mother owed her an explanation. This was too absurd.

She ran down with the file in hand, screaming loudly for her mom. "Mom, Mom, where are you? What is this? Mom, where are you??"

Jaya was practicing yoga on a large blue mat in the middle of their living room. Mina burst into the room.

"Why, Mom? What the hell is this? You used a sperm donor? I came out of a damn doctor's office? Could you not find a man? Why another woman's eggs? Do I have no part of you? Who am I, Mother? Who the hell am I?" She flung the folder into Jaya's face and then without waiting for a response, ran out of the house screaming. She found her bike on the front lawn, got on it, and biked away. She could hear her mother calling out behind her, running on the sidewalk, trying to catch up to the bike.

"Wait, Mina, honey, wait, I can explain, Mina!!!!"

But Mina did not stop. There was nothing Jaya could say to make this right. *I am a science experiment, a goddamn science experiment. I came out of a tube, out of a damn tube.*

When Mina returned home an hour later, she found the outside of the house crawling with firemen, an ambulance, and about half a dozen cops. The sirens were wailing and the neighbors were out. She jumped off her bike and tried to run past the wall of people into her house. No one would let her go in.

"Mom, Mom, where are you?" she yelled into the loud crowd. Finally, she ran up to one of the officers. "I live here. What happened?"

The frazzled-looking officer stared at her for a moment, "What is your name?"

"My name is Mina, I live here with my mom."

The officer was quiet.

"Is my mother okay? What happened? TELL ME NOW."

The officer gently pulled her into the house and shut the door. He walked her into the living room filled with more cops.

"This is the daughter. Her name is Mina," he said simply.

An older woman cop came up to Mina and said, "Come here, dear. Please come and sit down. Do you need a glass of water? Is there any other adult in the house? Does your father live with you?"

"I don't want to sit down. Where is my mother? What are you people doing here? What the hell is going on?"

"Your mother ... em ... I am sorry to tell you this, but your mother had an accident. We talked to your next-door neighbor. It appears she was running outside when she tripped right over there by the sidewalk and her head hit the large boulders out there by the garden. She was found lying on the road. Is there another adult we can talk to?"

"Where is she? What hospital did you take her to? Please, please tell me, I want to see her. NOW." Mina was screaming and starting to weep at the same time.

"Mina, I am afraid she did not make it. It appears the angle at which she hit the boulder broke her neck. She was not breathing when we got here. I am so sorry," the lady cop said with as much gentleness as she could muster.

"Dead? My mother is dead? Is that what you are telling me? My mother died chasing me down the street. Is that what you are telling me? Oh my God, my mother's dead?! That is not true.... it can't be ... she was just here practicing yoga ... right there on the carpet where you are standing ... please tell me it isn't true ... she is okay, right? I ... my mother is all I have ... please tell me she is okay ... no, no ... Mom ... oh God ... Mom."

Mina remembered nothing else of the night. She passed out soon after.

The next thing she remembered was waking up at the hospital, her grandmother Emmani sitting by her bedside. "Are you okay, Mina, honey? We have been so worried about you. Are you okay? Please talk to me .... Child ... are you okay? It's going to be fine ... our merciful God will take care of us. Come, let's pray for Jaya. It will be fine, child, I promise."

Mina stared at her blankly. Nothing was the same from that day on. Grandma Emmani moved into the tiny Bethesda home to take care of Mina. There were no more board games, no more midnight runs to Baskin-Robbins. Mina often gazed longingly at the list of places she and Jaya would have visited if all had been well. Now that would never be the case.

She started her poetry journal that year. Her first entry reflected her rendition of a song by singer famous at the time, Pankaj Udhas:

Looks like fun
A castle of mirrors
I go in and stare
Terror fills my heart
All the mirrors they stare at me
With faces that resemble mine
Friends or foes?
I stare hard to find a sign
I go and touch the mirrors
The faces they smile
No light in the eyes
No warmth in their smile

I scratch them with my fingers
The smiles widen
I begin to pound them with my fists
The smiles turn into laughter
I stop pounding and stare
The laughter stops, the faces in all shapes and sizes stare back
    intently at me
Then, I recognize it—that smile
I saw it in the mirrors, I saw it in their eyes
My death-wish grin

Grandma Emmani offered comfort and a gentle love. Mina missed her mother, always feeling responsible for Jaya's untimely accidental death.

After finishing high school, Mina signed up for and them promptly dropped out of George Washington University where she had enrolled for a degree in English literature. Emmani never asked why.

Mina began to work at a shelter in Northeast DC, working with battered women and their children, trying to find them homes, trying to find people with more pain than she was in. Her pain shrouded her being constantly, the thoughts of her mother "falling" and breaking her neck paralyzed her spirits. She constantly questioned the sperm and egg donor idea, often asking her grandmother why. "Your mother was a proud lady, Mina. Her ovaries were not producing good eggs so she got a donor. She had no time for the men in her life and so she got a donor. All she ever wanted was you, a child to love and call her own. Her methods you may not agree with, but child, her love was real. You are real. She loved you a lot." That answer never satisfied her—she often wondered who her father was, who was this man with a near-genius IQ and why was he donating his seed. The feeling of not knowing where she came from disabled her spirits on many mornings, often making it impossible to get out of bed.

Why did she not have a father? Who was her biological mother? How could her mother leave her like this? Why did she not deserve a family? What had she done? She never found the answers she needed but she did find the white powder that made her forget the questions.

It began with Tony. Tall, handsome Tony with this crazy blond hair, his six-pack abs, his intense drive to participate in every Iron Man competition he could get to. He was the director at the shelter she worked in.

"I don't normally do this, but would you like to have drinks with me?" Tony asked her on her second day at work, clearly smitten by her good looks and her smile.

"Well, you are the boss so how can I say no?" Mina had responded with a smile.

It was a slow-blossoming friendship until one evening when a bottle of wine went straight to Mina's head. That night she told him about her mother's death, her loneliness and her pain.

"I am here for you. I understand these things are not easy. Why don't you come with me to workout. I am not saying it will solve your problems but you know it will give your energy a place to go …," he offered and she had laughed at him.

"Workout? You think this will be solved by working out?"

They continued going out to lunch and the occasional dinner but she kept her physical distance from him.

One evening he found her at her desk, weeping.

"What is the matter? What happened?"

"It is Mom's death anniversary. I just don't want to go home. I just wish I could disappear. It has been five years. It still hurts so much," Mina said wiping her tears.

"Come on, come with me. I am going out with some friends tonight. It will distract you," Tony walked over to her, gently pulled her chair back and extended his hand.

She took it.

A year from now, this would be the moment he would regret forever.

At the club, things were loud, noisy, crazy. Tony ran into his old college crowd. They were drinking and smoking. One of them walked over to Mina and offered her a smoke. "No, don't give her that stuff, man, she doesn't do that," Tony pushed his friend away.

"Oh, you her mouthpiece? Let her tell me that! Girl, one whiff of this baby and you will be in heaven. You tell me that you still do not want to try this stuff?" The guy pushed the joint toward Mina.

With memories of her mother pushing her mind into dark places, Mina grabbed the joint and pushed Tony away.

The feeling that took over her made her feel like she could fly. And there was no looking back.

"I can fly, Tony," she said after fifteen minutes. "I can fly," she said, and jumped off the top of a table and broke her ankle.

The thought of her broken ankle brought her back to her painful cramps; her body was resisting the withdrawal and punishing her for it. It ached; it cried out for solace, it cried out for the whiffs that brought oblivion and freedom from her mind. She began to throw up again, and again, and again. There was nothing left in her stomach to vomit, yet the sensation just grew stronger and stronger and stronger.

"Open the door, Mina, open the door, this is fucking barbaric. Let me take you to a doctor," Tony yelled.

She kept the door locked. "If you love me, you will let me do this. Do you hear me? I have to do this now."

The screams started at midnight. They let the poison out of her system. As she yelled and screamed inside her room, she banged on the locked door. The door she had locked from the inside.

"Open the damn door, Tony, I don't want to do this anymore. Open it, I tell you. Who the hell gave you permission to lock it from the outside? Who are you to do this? This is my house, you hear me, it is my house, open the damn door. Who the hell do you think you are?" The demons screamed from inside her, pleading to be let out, to reign, to show everyone who was boss.

She realized at that point that she had locked the door and opened it. He was standing right outside. She lunged toward him, in anger and angst. Her knuckles were raw from banging at the door. He tried to hold her back. She turned wild, almost maniacal, and bit his wrist. A bite that would never really heal;

a bite that would throb years later at the mere mention of her name.

He managed to push her in and shut the door again. The screams turned to yelps, and the yelps to pleading, to begging. She wanted him to open the door. He would not. He wanted to, but it was not time yet. He held the door shut as she tried to pull it and open it. As the demons left her, she began to calm down. Then there was silence.

Tony worried about her. She had been this way for a year now. The drugs had changed her life. She wasn't the same person he had fallen in love with when he first laid eyes on her.

"It's love at first sight, Mina, I am gonna marry you someday," he told her.

"Is it love at first sight or lust at first sight?" she teased.

She treated him as a friend, but tonight, he knew it would change. Tonight with her drug purge, he was going to be her savior. He blamed himself for her getting introduced to the drugs. But now, he would be the one getting her off of them. It would show her how much he loved her, how he adored everything about her. Yes, indeed, he was going to save her.

Tony knew drugs played tricks on her mind and she did not even realize it. She was always concerned that the cops were following them wherever they went. The cops wanted to arrest her for killing her mother. She swore they hid behind trees, they hid behind cars, and even under her bed. He never saw any cops. He remembered the crumbled piece of paper he had found under her bed on one of the many nights she had passed out from the drugs. Her words, hidden in the crevices of the crumbled paper, seemed to have nowhere to go.

My smiles are carved, I hide behind their charade.
My smiles are carved, they hide my fear, my fate.
My smiles are carved, they hide my sins.
A loss to life is nothing new.
It is my death-wish grin.

The words, which had nowhere to go, went to his soul and haunted him.

One of her poems he had managed to save, one crumpled paper that she never did find him stealing.

Death feels I know no shame, for I call it as if it were my lover.
Death knows not my life is but a sham and I need it for my
heartaches to cover.
Loneliness feels I treat it like an old flame, who's come back
again to ease away the pain.
Loneliness knows not why and how I live, no wild emotions or
ambitions to tame.
Life feels I treat it like a betrayed love.
I treasure it not, then what for do I live.
Living and existing are two different things.
I exist, I do, I barely cling.

There is a fine line between living and existing and exist she did. On some days, barely. Those were her lines, not his. She was not a poet, she would tell him, yet her words were lyrical. Lyrical and chilling.

Tony kept the poem, rereading it each day. Trying to find a way to help her let the pain out, trying to find a way into that heart that seemed so closed to every emotion other than pure despair.

Recently, her drug use had spiraled out of control.

Tony no longer found crumpled papers.

It had been three hours since the screaming stopped. Tony was worried. He could not hear a sound. Perhaps, he thought, she had fallen asleep. He waited for another hour, pacing the room, running his hands through his wavy blond hair. His legs still hurt but all that seemed inappropriate to even think about at a time like this. He had no desire to sleep, the adrenaline was pumping and he could feel his pulse racing. Finally at around four in the morning, he decided to open the door.

She was not on the bed. The room was gently lit with a small lamp. The comforter was thrown on the floor along with pictures, papers, books, lipsticks. On the bed was a folder titled, "Mom and Mina's 100 places to visit before we die." And a few small, empty bottles of vodka. *Christ, where had she hidden the alcohol?*

"Mina," he whispered gently. "Are you okay?"

His blue eyes turned to look at the bathroom door. It was slightly open and he could see a light on. He slowly walked over, fearful of what he might find. As he opened the door, the smell overpowered him before he even saw her. Completely nude, she was sitting all curled up with her knees drawn to her chin and her head buried in her knees, on the side of the pale cream bathtub. She was seated in pools of vomit, covered with smatterings of fecal matter and splotches of blood. A small pocket knife lay but he could not see any large cuts on her body.

Tony tried to move forward to help her.

He stretched his arm forward. "Mina, honey, are you okay, can you hear me?" She barely nodded. As she moved, he saw small cuts on her legs with dried blood. He began to tremble. He thought she had stopped cutting herself a year ago. She had promised.

How could I trust a junkie, she never stopped anything, he thought as he moved forward to pick her up, trying to avoid stepping into the shit on the floor. He pulled her up. She was clutching what appeared to be a birthday card in her hand. He pulled it free. It was a card Jaya had written to Mina, probably many years ago. He placed the card on the bathroom sink. Mina shook slightly as if trying to awaken from her self-loathing stupor.

"Who is this? Why are you here? Mama, look, I made a mess. Mama, where are you? Mama, I am so tired," she slurred.

He supported her back with one arm and walked her into the shower stall. He held her close and turned the shower on full flow. The hot water washed off the shroud of human excretions. Mina seemed oblivious to the hot water and murmured, "Mom, Mom, I miss you. I am so sorry ... sorry, so sorry."

After the shower, he brought her back to her room and sat her down on the bed. "I'll be right back, honey," he whispered and rushed, dripping wet, to the linen closet just outside her room to find a couple of dry towels. He took off his jeans and t-shirt and wrapped a towel around himself and then headed to her.

"Put your towel on before helping the child in the seat next to you," he joked and in spite of the seriousness of the situation, he tried to make her laugh.

She was sitting still on the edge of the bed, dripping water everywhere. Quickly he dried her and got her dressed in a white t-shirt and, with some effort, clean underwear, and a blue skirt with an elastic waist. He lay her down and then went to dry himself totally and changed into a set of stinking sweats that were in the gym bag he had with him.

He came back into the room and lay down next to her on the bed.

"What now, Mina? Where do we go from here?" he said not quite loud enough for her to hear. Then louder, "Mina, would you like some water? Some coffee?"

She nodded and he headed to the kitchen to start the coffee machine.

As he began to start the machine, he remembered something, dropped everything he was doing, and sprinted back into her bathroom. The small knife was lying innocently on the bathroom floor where she had left it. He picked it up and took it back with him into the kitchen.

She was lying still on the bed, staring at the ceiling and clutching on to the folder he had seen on the bed earlier, along with the card from the bathroom.

It was around 6:00 am and they sat at her dining table sipping black coffee, the air thick with the aroma of the brew.

"I am going to call Nelson at the center," he said gently, worried about her reaction to the mere mention of his friend who worked the local rehab center. "Is that okay?"

"I …," she whispered.

"You need to take care of yourself now, please. No two ways about it—okay?"

She simply nodded, then got up and went back and lay down on her bed, shivering. He covered her with blankets and lay down next to her, holding her close. They both fell into a deep sleep.

At 8:00 am, Tony woke up and called Nelson, who promised to come and pick her up within the hour.

She emerged at around nine, looking strangely peaceful.

The doorbell rang, and Nelson walked into the house. "Mina, are you ready to go?" She nodded. He picked up her small bag.

"I will wait for you outside. Tony, thanks for calling me. Don't worry, we will take good care of her."

She handed Tony a piece of paper, neatly folded. "This is for you," she said quietly. "For all your help. Just lock up and keep the keys. You know where to find me …"

"Don't worry, I will pick up the mail and stop the paper. Eh, I will be here when you get back. Don't you worry," Tony said, wishing he had better, more insightful, more meaningful words to say to her.

She leaned over and kissed his forehead. "Thank you, Tony, for everything. I do love you, you know."

With that she was gone. He turned to go back into the house and then remembered the paper in his hand.

He opened it. The writing was messy, he could barely make out the words:

Walk carefully
My broken dreams lie all around
Remnants
Of longings
Of a life that never was
Of dignity lost and fame never found
The broken pieces, they prick my feet as I walk
The shards getting in between my toes
I stumble, I fall
They pierce my back, my fingers, my hands, my arms
My soul drips out—a drop at a time
Walk carefully, leave tomorrow but today be near
The time for us to bid goodbye is here.

His fingers shook as he folded the paper, his eyes brimming with tears. She really needed help, help that he could no longer provide.

"I forgot my purse," Mina said.

He turned around to see her standing behind him.

"Hold on, I will get it for you," Tony walked into the bedroom. As he picked up her purse, he noticed another piece of paper carelessly crumpled and thrown on the side. He picked it up. "I want you to meet a friend of mine …" it read, but before he could read it all, he heard Nelson calling. They needed to leave now. He put the paper in his pocket.

"Can you come too, Tony?" she asked in a childlike whimper. "I am scared to go alone."

He opened his mouth to say yes, but Nelson shook his head, "You will be fine, Mina, come on, you come with me. You don't need Tony for this." It would only be a few months, Nelson assured her and she would be fine, for sure.

And with that, she climbed into a big white SUV and was gone.

Tony should have felt relieved. He should have felt thankful. She was ready to let go of the habit that had destroyed her. Yet, he was scared. He wondered what would happen when she was cured. Would she not need him anymore? The overwhelming feeling of not wanting her to be cured made him feel ashamed. "You don't need Tony for this," Nelson's words rang in his ears. No, he thought, she does not need me.

He could not, he knew deep inside, wait for her anymore.

His love would not be able to bear the stresses of not being needed, of never being whole.

He turned to go back into her house, to lock it up one final time.

He left with the crumpled piece of paper, a bite mark on his wrist, and scream-filled nightmares to last him a lifetime.

He never imagined that her last verses on the crumpled paper, intended for herself, would become his destiny.

I want you to meet a friend of mine, to me who is very dear.
We've been friends for all our lives.
He never ever leaves my side, such loyalty I have never seen.
With him, I am never alone; he's been everywhere I have been.
I love my friend, who is so true. Listen, won't you meet him
    too.
He's promised me his friendship 'til after death.
You want his name?
Well, it's loneliness.

True Love

Georgetown, Washington, D.C.

"Thanks, Mrs. Carter, is there anything else I can get you?" Yuhiho said, smiling at the stylishly dressed, middle-aged woman. Mrs. Carter came in every week to buy just four cookies—two for herself and two special ones for her dog.

"Thanks dear, you are such a sweet girl. So responsible at such a young age! Not like my children, they are twenty and still ... well, I guess everyone is different," the lady smiled approvingly through her perfect dentures and then turned around and left.

Yuhiho hurried to lock up. She could not wait to close the store and start her special night. He had finally asked her out. Her red silk blouse and black skirt were ready, her nails were done, her long dark hair, usually straight, had been curled into large, bouncy ringlets, and she had even gotten permission from her mother to wax her arms and legs for the first time. "I wish I was old enough to get some eyelid surgery so my eyes would look like eyes instead of slits," she told her friends. But the doctor had said she was too young and to wait at least another five years. Well, for now she was as ready as she could be.

All she had to do now was close up the store and head home to have dinner and then get dressed.

She went back to the register to tally the day's receipts. The store, now in its third year, was doing well; actually, it was doing deliciously well. Yuhiho still remembered when the First Lady had come to the store, about six months ago or so, and ordered a large sample platter of Asian desserts, enough to feed a battalion. An item about this visit had made the style section of the *Washington Post* and there had been no looking back since. Several hundred people had stopped in the week the news hit and requested similar platters and several hundred more had stopped in since. It got so crazy the store created a platter called "The First Desserts" in honor of the First Lady: coconut jelly, sweet chocolate fortune cookies, almond won tons, honey sponge cake, white tea chocolate cake, and Vietnamese cold coffee cake.

The sales went through the roof as the store's popularity soared. Yes, business was good. It was funny, she never imagined this store would be so successful; Asian desserts, who would have thought that the Americans would fall in love with them considering no Asian restaurant she had ever been to offered a decent dessert menu.

The manager, Mr. Ishiguro, had left several hours ago to go to New York to bring in some new products. He had told her to wrap up the paper work and lock up for the night. She liked the fact that he trusted her and understood that she could handle the responsibility of the register and the store even though she was just sixteen.

It was already past eight and she was rushing to pack up the cookies when she saw the runner at the window. Yuhiho marveled that the runner always stood in the same spot outside as if she were replaying each day in the exact same way. She would always wave to Yuhiho and then run away before Yuhiho could invite her in. Yuhiho's bright black eyes smiled and shone even in the evening sun as she waved to the runner, a tall, slender girl with flowing dark hair.

With that, the runner waved and turned around and began to run in the opposite direction.

"Wait, wait!," Yuhiho kept calling. She wanted to offer the runner a few complimentary desserts. The girl always stopped and waved and never came in. Maybe a free taste will bring her in next time to buy something, Yuhiho reasoned with herself.

Yuhiho called out a few more times and then gave up and went back into the store, shaking her head in disbelief at the runner's rush. She remembered when she had told Mr. Ishiguro about the runner. "She sure runs fast," she had told him. "Why do you think she runs away from us, and so fast?" Yuhiho had asked.

"Perhaps, if she slows down, it will give her spirit a chance to catch up," he had whispered.

"What the hell does that mean," Yuhiho had muttered under her breath. He loved saying things that he thought sounded profound.

Yuhiho began to clean up the sample dessert plates and her mind pictured the runner's slender back as she ran with the wind. Just as Yuhiho walked toward the storage room to bring out for the items needed for the next day, her cell phone began to vibrate. It was Jack, "CU2nite." She smiled at the message, oh yes, she had big plans tonight. "GR8" she replied.

Tonight was about the party. With Jack, yes, Jack, baby blue eyes, blond hair, and all—the quintessential American hunk. It was going to be her first date, ever. She never really had an interest in boys until Jack approached her.

Jack's interest in her had sparked a pathetically childish outburst from her so-called friends. Earlier in the day, she was in a bathroom stall at school when she heard two of her "friends" chatting outside.

"Why on earth is Jack taking that Asian bitch to the party? I am so freaking pissed." "Yes," the other one added, "hasn't he noticed that the pimple-faced twit walks with one shoulder up higher than the other? SUB, you really did find the perfect name for her, SUB: shoulder-up bitch!"

"He must think she is a baller … she ain't nothing else, she ain't a looker and she ain't no genius, nothing."

"Maybe we can ask Jack and his friends to turn old slit-eyes into the Bukkake warrior. At least it will clear up her acne! Who ever heard of a Jap with such dark skin."

With that, they laughed and were gone. Yuhiho wanted to explain that she had her Japanese mother's features and her South Indian father's gorgeous dark complexion, she wanted to tell them what her mother had told her—that she was uniquely beautiful and there was no one quite like her. But instead, Yuhiho stayed in the stall and cried. These were the same girls she had homeroom with in the morning and they giggled with her as she told them how sweetly he had asked her out. And here they were planning on asking Jack and his friends to ejaculate all over her face. When she walked out of the bathroom, Jack was standing outside, waiting for her, "Hey Yuhiho ... can I give you a ride home? I got my dad's car but it's parked way out in friggin' Bumblefuck." She laughed.

He was so sweet. His family had just moved into their neighborhood about three weeks ago and lived three houses down from her.

"If you don't mind, I will take the bus," she said shyly.

"Okay. Have it your way, I will join you and come back for my car later."

As the coolest, most handsome boy in school walked her to the bus at school, she discretely flipped her hair and turned her head. Yes, they were watching, those damn little witches: her "friends." Serves them right, they could never have him now, she had no intention of ever letting him go.

He led her onto the bus, brushing against her just so. They climbed in together, sat together in an awkward silence in the otherwise noisy bus. He sat close enough that she could smell his cologne, or was it his masculine scent? In just a few minutes they were at her bus stop.

They walked together toward her Cape Cod–style house, a mere block from the bus stop. He held her hand. Another first for her.

As they turned the corner onto her picturesque street, he stopped. It was a wooded, quiet, and secluded street. They both knew it well—she from playing in the streets for over fifteen years, and he from exploring it over the past few weeks.

Gently, he pulled her towards him and brushed his soft lips first against her forehead and then pressed them onto her lips. He pulled away and smiled at her, his eyes twinkling with mischief. She was completely stunned. Her first kiss with a boy and it was over before she knew it. Wasn't the earth supposed to move and her heart supposed to race? She smiled nervously at him, hoping that he had not noticed that she felt nothing.

"I have to go now. I have to go to work in Georgetown," she said to him.

"I will see you tonight, beautiful," he said and then blew her another kiss and left.

I just got caught off-guard, that's all, she thought. Tonight will be the real thing. She threw her bag just near the front door and rang the bell, *"Okasaan,* I am late, please take this bag." Without waiting for her mother to respond, she got on her hot pink bike and began to ride furiously toward Georgetown. She had promised Mr. Ishiguro she would be early today.

The afternoon flew by as she dreamt of what the evening had in store.

Now, she looked around the store one final time to make sure that she had cleaned up properly, put things back where they belonged and locked the front door. Mr. Ishiguro was a stickler for details. Satisfied, she turned off the lights and turned on the alarm. She locked the service door and got back on her bike to ride home.

As she entered the house, her mother appeared.

"I'm home, okaasan."

"O-kaeri nasai," came the gentle response. Her mother had perfected the art of being seen and not heard. It drove Yuhiho nuts that Mother would never wave her arms, raise her voice, laugh out loud, or even cry. She was a Japanese doll, a *kokishi*—perfectly carved with features painted on—and she hid behind a cultural veil that even Yuhiho could not penetrate.

Self-consciously, Yuhiho straightened her hair with her hands and smoothed out her clothes. She was sure her mother would be able to sense that she had been kissed. "How do you know so much about me, *okaasan?*" she often asked. "How did you know I had ice cream at midnight last night or that I called Sheryl seventeen times today?" Her mother would always nod and smile. Occasionally, the smile even seemed real. Very occasionally.

Yuhiho stared at her mother, ready to spill her heart—*I had my first kiss today, Mamma. It was so cool. He kissed me! Jack actually kissed me.* "Did you have a good day at work? Would you like some Homo sausage?" her mother asked as she made her way into the kitchen.

"The name is funny, okaasan, Homo sausage!" Yuhiho laughed.

"*Ii kagen ni shinasai, Yuhiho,*" her mother exclaimed.

"What do you mean, behave properly? It is funny, come on, admit it."

Her mother smiled and gave her a plate of sausage and cheese. As Yuhiho ate, she watched her mother's face carefully. She could not believe her mother had not sensed anything yet, how could she not have sensed Yuhiho's first kiss? Part of her was thankful, another part annoyed. But Mom would not understand anyway, she thought, she's too old, has been married too long, and is way too Japanese.

Her mother began the elaborate ritual of serving dinner. Each night, dinner was a production.

Japanese women are supposed to be the epitome of grace yet her mother was a complete klutz. Chipped dinnerware, mismatched flatware, and even droplets of tea in the tray as she tried to master the art of tea service. Sometimes Mom would rotate the bowl in the wrong direction and droplets of tea could fly out of the bowl when she would whisk it. Yes, her mother, the klutz, the *don-kusai*. Her Indian father, thanks to his obsessive love for his wife, had perfected the art of overlooking his wife's faults and pretended not to notice. It certainly was not for lack of trying, but she just did not have it. She made up for her inelegant ways by being a fabulous cook. Tonight's dinner was a testament to her art in the kitchen. Miso soup. The perfectly simmered *niku jyaga* (meat and potatoes) and *yakinasu* (eggplant) were Yuhiho's favorite. And, of course, sticky rice.

After a quiet, conversationless dinner with both her parents, she excused herself. "I am tired tonight, I am heading to bed."

"Please help your mother with the dishes first," her father said and then retired to the living room to watch the BBC. Over the clinking of the dishes as she put them in the dishwasher, her mind wandered to what was going to happen at the party. She could barely hold in her excitement. "Why are you so distracted, Yuhiho? Please look at the mess you are making with the dishes. Go on, go to bed. I will clear this," her mother gently pushed her away from the dishwasher and took over the task.

Yuhiho ran up the stairs to her room and shut the door. She had an hour to get dressed and leave, or rather sneak out. She could hear her parents winding down and finally heard her dad turn off the TV and retire to his room for the night.

She quickly got dressed and applied her mineral makeup. The ads on TV had promised flawless skin. She was pleased with the result: the pimples no longer looked red and her skin appeared less blotchy.

Quietly she opened the tiny window over the bathtub in her bathroom and cautiously stuck her head out to see if Jack was outside waiting. The cool air assaulted her face. Then she saw him, yes, standing in the shadows, it was him.

She climbed down the window and jumped down ten feet. Having done this many times before, she knew exactly where to step on the ledge below the window and exactly how to jump so she did not break anything or rip her dress. It had been hard explaining to her father how she broke her ankle in the middle of the night a few months ago. He seemed to buy the story that she fell of the bed. But surely he wouldn't buy it again.

Hand in hand, Yuhiho and Jack headed to the party at his friend's house. Blaring eighties-style music, thick cigarette smoke, and hordes of kids greeted them at the door. "Can you believe they are playing Michael Jackson?" he said. She smiled and took off her jacket. They got herded in and on to the living room, cleared out to serve as a dance floor.

A drink showed up from somewhere in her hand, she sipped it tentatively. It tasted nonalcoholic and she was relieved; at the last party someone had spiked it without telling her. Hangovers were not her thing; she hated them and was sure her mother could tell the next morning.

The music changed from the foot tapping song to an oldie—a slow George Michael number. Jack took the drink from her hand and put it on a counter nearby, then pulled her onto the dance floor.

He pulled her close and she felt his breath on her neck. They moved to the music and everything around them seemed to slow down to match their pace. Everyone smiled at them with knowing glances. He smiled back at them. She wondered if this was it. He seemed nice enough but something seemed amiss, she could not quite put her finger on it. She ought to be thrilled, she was the center of attention and certainly the object of envy at this party, but something did not quite feel right.

"Change the damn song," someone screamed over the sensual careless whispers of George Michael, and New Republic came on. Jack turned to her and smiled. He gave her a peck on the cheek and then signaled that he was going to go out for a quick smoke.

She looked around to see if she could figure out where Jack had put her drink. All of a sudden she felt someone grab hold of her arm and pull her onto the dance floor. Yuhiho was startled and began to pull away. She was here with Jack. What would people think if they saw her with another dancer? The dancer would not let go of her arm and pulled her closer and closer.

Yuhiho stopped resisting.

The other dancer moved sensually, slowly, sliding up close and pulling away just so. The dancer's body was rhythmic, moving to the music, one with the sound. Yuhiho found herself being led into making moves she did not know her body could make. The dancer twirled her around and pulled her close. She began to giggle and then laugh. This felt right to her, so much better than with Jack. This had the feeling of closeness, of togetherness, that she found lacking with him. The lights went down again and the music slowed. The dancer pulled her into a dark corner. She felt a kiss being planted on her lips.

Instantly, Yuhiho knew this was it. This is what she always wanted. This was the kiss that had been missing. This is what she had been longing for.

The song was finished and the lights came back on. Yuhiho pulled away, looking around to see if Jack had seen her and then used her hands to hide her face.

But the dancer would not let go and grabbed her arm again. This time, instead of the dance floor, the dancer pulled her and led her into the bathroom and shut the door. The dancer pushed Yuhiho against the dark-paneled door of the bathroom and she could feel her clothes begin to get pulled at and removed. The dancer's hands explored every inch of Yuhiho's young body. Yuhiho tried resisting, "No, this isn't right."

The dancer pulled back, "Why?"

How could she answer the why? Yuhiho knew the dancer well. They went to the same school. The dancer was in the same grade. They exchanged glances in the hallways, they smiled at each other in homeroom, they managed to bump into each other at the library all the time.

Yuhiho wanted to shout, "Because this is love that can never be whole. It's a love that will never be fulfilled. My parents, what will they say." Her conservative parents would be shamed and lose face.

She pulled away from the dancer, her clothes in disarray, her silk shirt wrinkled.

The dancer let go.

Yuhiho found Jack on the dance floor, looking for her. "What happened to your clothes?" he asked.

"Nothing, nothing," she said. "Can you take me home, please?"

She opened the front door with the spare key. With her parents sleeping, she was sure that no one would notice her. As soon as she opened the door, she knew she was busted. She could hear voices and see lights in the living room.

As she closed the front door, she could sense her father had come out of the living room and was standing behind her.

"Yuhiho, where have you been?" He was livid but whispered his words.

"Yuhiho, answer me. Where have you been? How dare you sneak out of the house? How dare you leave the house at this hour of night? And, and you are smelling of beer and cigarettes. Have you been smoking? Answer me, young lady!" his voice now bellowed.

Yuhiho just stood there looking down at her shoes.

"And your clothes? What happened to your clothes? Why are they all messed up? Your blouse looks ripped on the side. Did a boy do this to you? Were you out with a boy?" her father continued to yell as her mother stood in the shadows and watched quietly.

"Answer me—what did the boy do to you?"

"Nothing, father. The boy did nothing. I am sorry I went out. It won't happen again."

"Why do you lie to me, Yuhiho? You think I do not know that you sneak out? I am not blind, deaf, and dumb. I know what goes on in this house. I can smell the boy on you and you say nothing happened."

"I do not lie, father. Nothing happened with him."

"We will discuss it later, Yuhiho. Now go to bed. You disrespect me by lying to me. Go to your room."

"I do not lie, father, it was not a boy," she mumbled and quietly went up to her room.

The Prize of War

The headstone was cold, white and cold. Zara hugged it, clutching the gold pendant in her hand. The slithering, chilly breeze, funneling through the gravestones, added to the misery of the evening. The tourist buses were all gone. The guards had changed for the last time that day and no rifle sounds could be heard anymore.

Death is quiet.

Friends, loved ones, even some enemies had come for the funeral.

They had said their tearful, some even heartfelt, goodbyes, recalled his life as they admired his shiny coffin, all ready for the final goodbye.

Then they left.

They left him alone in the ground to be forgotten as they went on with more important things: When does the next episode of *Idol* air? What time is the Justin Timberlake concert? Have you tried that new Asian restaurant at the Penn Quarter?

It had been two weeks since the funeral.

Two long weeks and she came every day to the Arlington Cemetery to say goodbye to Robert McKenzie Young. Twenty-five and dead. Dead before life even began. Dead before their wedding. Dead before their babies could be born. Dead before his time, before their time, before he even knew what he was going to do with his life. She had just decided to tell the world about him. She was going to tell her mother and her father. Everyone was going to know that she had finally settled down and found the perfect soul mate. But life had other ideas. There are few people in this world who get all they want. *The rest of us just have to pretend*, she thought bitterly, *to appreciate and love this gift of being alive.* Even on days like today, when life seemed nothing more than a burden to be carried.

Her last communication with him had been a month or so ago. His task in the war-torn zone was to go door to door through the villages looking for insurgents.

"How will you know? No one has a label on their forehead, 'I am a terrorist, come get me.' How will you know if it is a man just protecting his family with his guns rather than an insurgent waiting to kill all American peacekeepers who come his way?" she wrote in a note to him.

His reply frightened her even more. He sent a note asking her to send him flashlights, batteries, gum, and warm blankets for the upcoming winter months.

"There is nothing here except dust and sadness, there is so much poverty in the villages, it's unbelievable. It is strange, this tour of duty—I know we are trying to help them, we are here to enforce peace but what they need here is more food and less guns and less bullets. Zara, it will shock you—I have met families who are surviving on rotting bread, teaspoons of old oil, and absolutely disgusting water—you can't even tell that it is water—it has so many gross things floating in it. Water tankers are supposed to bring water but all the roads are closed. The people are depending on rivers that are almost completely dry in this horrendous August heat. I break down their doors and point guns at them. They look at my water bottles with big, sad eyes. I am so torn between service to my country and what I see here on the ground. I have heard of girls being gang-raped in what is supposed to be temporary housing to help them find shelter, little boys carrying guns like they are baseball bats to play games, old women being dragged out of their homes by their hair, men being shot in the genitals—I could never have imagined that the human race is a capable of such evil."

Reading his note made her shake. This was a country, post war, where the American and European peacekeepers were sent in to make sure no radical groups caused trouble again. She could tell Bob was frustrated at not being able to help in a way that made him feel like he made a difference. She read on:

"Nick Dani, one of my buddies, has a wife at home about to give birth and yet here we don't know if we will live from one moment to the next. Last night in one of the local homes, the richest in the village, a mother and her young sons offered us a bowl of yogurt and a cool glass of lemonade—I thought I had died and gone to heaven. My throat is still not used to all the dust storms and I have developed a nasty hack. I feel like an asshole for even complaining about such petty things when people here are dying of malnutrition and starvation. Oh, and the answer to the million dollar question—have we found any insurgents yet? I am not sure. I cannot define an insurgent anymore. Are they the radicals trying to kill us or the locals trying to get freedom from their own government—does that make them insurgents? I do my job and my duty but I question my spirit constantly.

"They tell me it's for peace. All I see is poverty. What right do I have to be here? I don't understand this. I don't want to understand this anymore. I just want to come home. I try to sleep and pray that when I wake up this nightmare is gone. But it is here and it is real. It won't end. I used to look to the sky for hope and love. I can't now. I suffocate under this sky. Their sun does not want me here. It does not welcome me. It burns through my clothes, my skin. It pierces my heart. I ask for forgiveness each night for all the sins I am committing. I ask for forgiveness from Christ and from the Allah. One of them will forgive me ... although I doubt it. I came here to help and I can do nothing.

"I am not sure how much longer I can do this. Starved bodies are rotting on sidewalks, children are playing near shrapnel, and there seems to be no hope in sight—for them or us. Zara—I wish I could speak some of the local dialect. Damn it, why didn't I learn? I wish I could speak even a few words, I think it would help us connect so much with the people here. I have to go now. I love you, Zara and cannot wait to come home. I feel like I am living a nightmare. God help us all. Yours, Bob. P.S. As a kid, I always dreamt of sleeping under the stars. I just never imagined that it would be under an open desert sky with an artillery lullaby."

The note had arrived in August and she mailed a care package for him and his friends within a day, adding granola bars, beef jerky, warm socks, and different varieties of small hard candy that he could carry easily in his pocket and share with his buddies.

A week later, another note arrived. It looked like it had been mailed from downtown Washington, DC. This time it was not just from him. The envelope was heavy and she could feel something hard inside. She did not recognize the handwriting on the cover.

She brought the envelope in with her to her apartment and sat down on her couch. Slowly, she opened it. A gold cross fell out. No, no, it couldn't be, she thought. With quivering, shaking fingers she picked it up: Bob's gold cross. She could hear her own breaths, coming now in short spurts. She gently placed the cross on her lap and looked back in the envelope. There was a neatly folded note. She knew what it was even before reading it.

Instantly she recognized Bob's handwriting.

"Zara, my darling: I wrote this on an impulse thinking 'what if.' If you are reading this, my dearest Zara, it means I did not make it. In both our hearts, we knew this could happen. Always know that I am with you and I love you. You completed my life and made it worth living. Don't cry for me. Smile and I will be forever in your heart. Yours always, Bob."

At first the note seemed like somebody's idea of a cruel joke.

There was another note inside the envelope. This was no joke, but it was cruel.

"Zara, my name is Nick Dani and I am friend of Robert's. I am so very sorry to tell you this but Robert was killed by a stray bullet. We were in a peacekeeping zone but sometimes gun fights do break out. I apologize for the abruptness of this note but things here are not safe at the moment and I want to send this note with the team heading back today to the US. He loved you very much and spoke of you often. I thought you might want his cross. He loved you."

She cried for hours and then put the cross and the note in her purse.

Perhaps this Nick Dani was mistaken and Bob was not the one who was killed. Perhaps. She walked around in a daze for about a week. She could barely sleep at night, barely stay awake in the day. Her sister constantly called to ask her what was wrong. She wanted to share, she so wanted to share, but the words would not come out. Nothing would come out of her mouth. She was sad at first, and then angry with him. He had no right to die. What was going to happen to her? How dare he die and leave her alone? The anger helped her rationalize his death for a day or so. The anger dissipated and the sorrow returned when she got a call from someone sounding very official telling her that his body had arrived in the US.

After his body arrived, she began to sleep even less. He was home, yet he was never coming home. His body, or what was left of it, had arrived here, but his spirit, his soul, was lost somewhere in a desert on the other side of the world. What would his last moments have been like? Did he pray? Did he know he was going to die? Or was it instant, she wondered over and over again. What had his death accomplished? What was the moral of his story?

Red blotches appeared on her body, perhaps in reaction to the stress, but she could not tell what they were. They itched, they hurt. At night they seemed to burn through her body, then they went away.

She stared at the gravestones around her. Grass had grown over the graves in the past two weeks, there were fresh flowers placed near the many others. The cemetery was impeccably maintained—each blade of grass cut perfectly—a soothing, even picturesque setting that hid the pain and cruelty of death. She looked at the gravestone on the far right that had a beer can beside it, another one on the extreme right that had a box of Snickers bars placed near its edge, and one right behind Bob's that had a Redskins cap.

She wondered if he had fought with any of the men and women buried alongside. Did he know the people he had been laid to rest with? It was a strange phrase, "laid to rest"—how could he be resting when his life had been taken from him unexpectedly. How could he be resting when his soul was still wandering in a strange land.

Bob had lit up her life in more ways than one. He was the first man she ever loved, ever trusted. She had grown up under the dark shadows of her failure to protect her sister from sexual abuse at the hands of a stranger. But that stranger was not the ultimate sinner, she once told Bob, I am because I could have done something to stop it and I did not.

That abuse was a lifetime ago. Or did it just seem like it when the unthinkable happened.

She and her twin were seven then and it was the month of April. Their garden was in full bloom with azaleas, tulips, and impatiens peeking out from every nook and cranny. The gentle green of the leaves soothed the eyes. They loved playing in the sprinklers their dad would set up every evening for them. It was perfect, almost idyllic. Almost.

Each morning the girls would dress themselves, eat a banana, kiss their father and mother goodbye. The parents would leave for the office and the girls would pretend to wait for their nanny to walk them to the bus stop. The nanny had taught them the art of faking. Zara even to this day marveled at the fact that their parents never picked up on the nanny's sham. As soon as their parents would leave for work, the nanny would let them out of the house and tell them that they were old enough to walk by themselves and that they did not need her to walk them. Besides, she had better things to do than waste her time going to the bus stop. "Your Indian parents are too protective of their children. You need to be smart and go on your own. The stop is just a block away … now go there and don't behave like babies and ask me to come along, you don't need me. Go, go Zara and Ziya, go now or you will miss the bus."

The sisters would huddle close and walk to the bus stop about a block away from the house. They were the only two at the bus stop and often stood together, holding hands, and anxiously waiting for the bus to arrive. Although the area was beautiful, adorned with flowering plants of every color and shade imaginable, it was secluded and to Zara, it even seemed sinister on some days—especially when dark clouds covered the sky or there was so much snow on the ground, just walking to the bus stop was a hike.

About eight months into the second grade, the Pokemonster neighbor began to show up at the bus stop. Zara often referred to him as "Pokemonster" since he reminded them of a nasty Pokemon character. He usually did nothing but just stood there and stared at them. Zara hated his prying eyes—she could feel his stare go from the top of her head to the end of her toes. He just looked and smiled. And then looked some more.

One morning, he actually talked to them. "Hi, do you want to come and meet Peter Rabbit?" At first, her sister refused his offer to see the rabbit. He came back again the next day, this time with rabbit in hand. "Come here, see he is so cute! You will like him. Come on, let's go into the house and get him some carrots."

The rabbit was too cute for her sister to resist and the thought of feeding such a precious bundle made her forget about Pokemonster. Zara tried to stop her, "The bus is coming, please don't go." But she was gone.

Terror does not happen in dark alleys alone. On this day it was such a beautiful morning with a gloriously blue sky, singing robins, and blooming tulips.

The bus came. Zara kept calling to her sister but there was no sign of her. "Come on, let's go," said the bus driver. She boarded the bus and left her sister.

It was a decision she regretted forever.

When she returned that afternoon from school and the bus stopped at her stop, she got down and saw her sister sitting on the curb and crying. Her dress looked ruffled, her hair was messed up.

"What happened?" she asked gently, then put her arm around her sister. "What happened? Are you okay? He did not hurt you, did he? We can tell Dad and Dad will fix him. But please don't tell Mom, she will be so mad that I left you alone here. What happened?"

"Nothing, nothing happened. I won't tell Mom. Why did you not wait for me, Zara? Why did you leave me here alone? Why?"

The two girls skipped school for the next two days. They pretended to go to the bus stop, but would then go back to the house and hide in the small shed in the backyard.

The day they went back, one of the teachers sent a note home asking why the little girls had not been coming to school and why no one had bothered to call the school back.

Zara recalled the day with great agony.

The nanny read the note before the parents had a chance. "You girls, you must be up to no good. Where did you go? Okay, you won't tell me? Zara—I want to know where she was and I want to know now or I will break both your legs." She slapped Zara and then her sister, three, four times. On each cheek and then proceeded to pull them by their hair and drag them into Zara's room. The twins wept, first for themselves, and then for each other. The nanny tore the teacher's note and threw it in the trash. "Not one word to your father or your mother, you hear me? You are little bitches. Not one word to your father. I will come with you to the bus stop tomorrow so that you can no longer do this."

The nanny slammed the door, leaving the girls huddled on the floor. Years later, her sister told Zara, "I felt like I had been raped all over again."

For Zara, a lifelong nightmare had just begun.

"I should have done something, Bob, something, anything," Zara would constantly say.

"What could you do, Zara? You were a child."

"Bob, don't you envy people who wake up each day and want to face the day and say prayers of thanks? My prayer is so different. Remember that old children's prayer of 'Now I lay me down to sleep?'—mine was so different. *Now I lay me down to sleep, I pray for someone my soul to keep and I want to die before I wake so I pray for someone my soul to take.*"

Bob held her closer and she cried.

"I have had the same nightmare for the longest time. My sister is in the ground and looking up at me through some grate. I can see her hands coming out the grate and reaching, pleading, begging me to pull her out. I am standing by the grate but I cannot reach her. I am frozen. I try to reach, to hold her, to help her, to pull out the grate. I can't reach. I go closer and there is a snake sitting on the grate, hissing at me, I am terrified of snakes. Still I try but my arms are not long enough to reach. I keep bending down and the grates move further away. The snake keeps getting bigger and bigger and he lunges at me. I leave her there and run away. Each time. I run away. I am so ashamed." Bob held her as she cried and cried.

Twenty years of weeping had not lessened Zara's pain and she wondered why she even cried now. The wound was still as fresh today as it was years ago, infected and smelling, it had permeated every part of her soul, every part of her being.

Each time Zara looked at her sister's pained face it reminded her of her own failure. Her sister began to shrink into a quiet, almost destitute child. Zara became loud and outrageous.

Zara was beautiful and was approached to model for some local advertisers. Her first stint was to act as a "happy consumer" in an ad for an Indian phone service provider. The agent getting her the deal promised her fame and glory for her looks and talent. She lost her virginity and any remaining self-respect to get the deal. It was followed by "Nude Lady 2 in Scene 6" of a B-grade movie, and then "Nude Lady Lying Down with Chicken Tikka on Her Stomach, Scene 96" for another one. Her movie career ended as it had begun—in the bed of a stranger.

Each month after that, there was a Tim who led to a Jim who led to a Rohan who led to a Mike in her life, all offering to take her to from Belize to Barbados, from St. Bart's to Alaska; to buy her a Gucci or Prada, to treat her to another wonder of the world. At first she was reluctant. Once she accepted, she knew it had nothing to do with who she was and everything to do with the physical appearance she had. All the men that she met wanted only one thing—to sleep with this angelic woman-child. She slept with them all, first date or not—what difference did it make? It all ended up the same way. When they got tired of her, they left.

"For such a sexy babe, you ain't much of a kisser," one disgusting man told her. Later when he thought she was sleeping, he called some friend on the phone. "She is a good fuck but that is it, man. You know me, man, cover the face and fuck the base, they are all the same. Asian ones are feisty."

She lost count of how many men there had been.

Her parents seemed proud of all her expensive jewelry and gifts, never once asking about the cost of it all.

The night she met Bob was the first night she ever kissed a man and meant it. Ever.

Bob had been different. They had met at a bookstore and he had asked her out. A few days later, on their first date, they had been sitting beside each other at a ritzy Georgetown bar. After a few hours of talking, he had simply leaned over and gently kissed her lips. It was the strangest feeling for her. It felt wonderful. It was painful and so beautiful. He seemed happy to be alive, thankful to be alive.

And now, he was gone.

She could never know what truly happened to Bob; she would have to take Nick Dani's version of the story.

She wished there was someone in his family she could call. Someone she could talk to about him, his life before her, his childhood.

She barely knew anything about his family. It was not a topic that he liked to discuss. He had lost his father many years ago and his sister was admitted full-time to a sanatorium. The questions she asked about his mother always went unanswered and finally she stopped asking. She figured Bob's friend Nick must have informed someone in the military to call her, or else how would they have contacted her about the funeral. There had been no family at his funeral. She was the only "family." There were a few of the young men he had served with. They all told her he loved her very much. She stood there stoically, not sure how to react. She thought that no one knew they had been in love for six months, from the night they met at the bookstore. Six months is a short time for some. For them it was a lifetime that started with a kiss and ended at his grave.

She came to the cemetery every day. She stopped going out, and on many days even stopped eating.

"Zara, you don't look so good. What is wrong? You have not been to see us? When are you coming over?" Her mother, sweet and kind as always, left her so many messages like that, Zara had lost count.

"I will tell you what is going on soon," she promised. *As soon as I can talk about it*, she thought to herself.

She began to weep again, holding the headstone closer and closer. "Bob, the blotches, the bumps are back on my hand. See here ... they won't go away. I called the doctor, they don't know what it is. A big blotch was on my back last week. It just won't go away. It itches and itches all day ... see, see how red it is." The blotches, real and imagined, appeared at times of high stress. Zara could feel them and see them. The doctors, or anyone else, could never see any blotch. They could only see where she had scratched so hard she had drawn blood.

The wind died down.

She held the stone close and looked up and around her. She noticed a few other souls hovering over the gravestones of their lost loved ones.

"Life is only precious when you start to lose it," her father said often. As a nurse in the ER, Zara knew he saw more than his fair share of death.

She opened the tiny bottle of vodka in her purse and gulped it down. It was her third small bottle of the day.

Suddenly, someone placed a hand on her shoulder.

Zara jerked and turned her head up.

"Sorry, I did not mean you startle you, child. I am Bob's mother. My name is Suzanna," said the elegant older woman dressed in a dark blue pant suit. "You must be Zara."

"Yes, I am Zara. I, I used to date Bob, I mean, we were engaged. I mean, I am so sorry about all this. I …"

Zara then struggled for words to explain why she had his ring on her finger but could not recognize her would-be mother-in-law. She felt compelled to tell this woman everything. She could not. The lady simply sat down next to her.

"It's okay, child. You don't have to explain anything. My son told me everything about you. He loved you a lot and told me he was going to marry you," the woman said, startling Zara.

"He told you? Really? We had decided to keep it quiet until he came home from his mission. I guess, he is home now."

The older woman managed a smile even as her green eyes, just like his green eyes, shimmered with tears.

"He promised to introduce you to us when he came home. He had told us he would be done with the Army so that we could all be a family."

He did come home, just a bit earlier, leaving his soul in the desert.

"Thank you for attending his funeral. I was away and could not make it. I am glad he was not alone when he was buried. I am glad you were with him."

Zara sobbed uncontrollably and then turned to hug the older woman. They began to talk. She told the woman about her life and Bob. Everything all came out together, jumbled, nothing was in sequence, nothing made sense, nothing seemed too small, she talked and talked.

Somewhere in the background she heard a bus start up. It startled her. She thought the buses were all gone but it appeared that the last of the tourists were leaving the cemetery to return to their lives. Lucky them, they had lives they could go back to. She preferred to stay with Bob. This was her life.

The older woman sat with her on the grass, held her hand, and listened. "He loved you and I love you for it. Just be strong."

After an hour, they hugged. The woman got up to leave.

"I will be back, I promise. But you must learn to get on with your own life. He is gone and he is not coming back. You will need to learn to move on, you are so young, child. He would have wanted you to be happy."

The woman reached in to her bag and pulled out a photograph. It was a picture of Bob in his uniform. "I thought you would like to have this," she said.

Zara took the photograph and bend down to kiss it. When she looked up, the woman was gone. She stood up and turned to walk towards the Arlington Metro stop. She had lived all her life in Washington, DC and had never visited the cemetery. It was one of those "someday I will do it" things. These soldiers had died, Robert had died, so people like her could live in peace. It was a high price to pay for existence. The wind was cold and stung her, reminding her of her loss. She had said her last goodbye to him. She knew in her heart now she would never be back. Her grief had been shared.

The leftover pain was now only hers to bear. Alone.

She walked toward the train. Her cell phone started to ring; it was her dad. "Zara, how are you? Mom is so worried, call her."

"I will, Dad." Zara said, fidgeting with the cell phone. The reception was really poor and she could barely walk two steps without tumbling. The vodka, thankfully, had taken over.

She walked toward the escalator for the Metro. A quiet ride brought her home to an even quieter apartment. She placed the cross and the photograph that she had been clutching all evening right next to the photo of her and Bob on her mantle.

The three-bedroom condo, with its olive green silk drapes, grandiose sofas upholstered with honey-hued raw silk textiles and cashmere throws were all paid for by men. She recoiled instinctively each time she touched anything. She had pledged that when she started her life with Bob, none of this would be around. They would go shopping at IKEA and build an affordable nest, one that was paid for by them and not their sins.

Hunger pangs reminded her that she had not eaten the whole day. The fridge was bare except for some leftover pizza. She heated it in the microwave and inhaled it along with some leftover red wine that would have been better poured down the drain.

Around 11:00 pm, she opened another bottle of vodka. Then began calling Bob's cell phone to hear his voice. He was gone but his voicemail was still there. She left messages on top of messages. *Call me back, I love you. Call me back, I miss you. Just call me.*

Around 2:00 am, she popped three Tylenol PM and after throwing off all her clothes on the floor, slipped into a dreamless sleep.

Suddenly, she bolted up straight. Was he really dead? Was this a nightmare?

Her memory was fuzzy, the vodka, the pills. Had she been to the cemetery last night? She shivered in bed as she tried to recall the events of the previous night. Nothing was clear. It was all muddled together. She stared at her clock. It was already five-thirty and the sun was peeking out, greeting the world, beckoning it to wake up to a glorious day.

She ran over to the mantel. His cross was still there. She could have sworn there was a picture of him in his youth, a photo of him wearing his uniform. But there wasn't. The only picture there was one of the two of them.

She smiled at the photograph of them together.

There was no escape but now, perhaps, there was no longer a need to escape.

The Vermillion Promise

Bethesda, Maryland

Nitin stood at the entrance of the house and removed his shoes. It was an old, ingrained habit. Dirty shoes drag in all that the world discards, his wife always said.

The noise outside was deafening. Their homeowners' association in Bethesda had just hired a new company to clean up the fall leaves, and the blowers were going at full speed. The light was fading. The sky, splashed with deep reds, yellows, and some blue, was beautiful as it paid homage to the earth.

He stared at the nameplate on the door—Nita and Nitin Singh. He gently ran his fingers over it.

"Dad, no one puts name plates on their doors," his youngest had quipped when Nitin first put the plate up. Nitin did not know how to explain to the youngster why this nameplate was so important. "Nita and Nitin Singh"—the words were his whole life. A nameplate on a house, a house he bought with his life savings, a house that housed his dreams, his life, and his love.

Flipping the light switch, Nitin entered the house and walked into the living room. He turned on all the lights. "Why do you need so much light?" Nita would have said. But that was him, every light in the house needed to be on when he was home.

The crystal on the table sparkled in the laser light of the spotlight Nita had arranged just for them. It was her pride and joy, this table. He joked that it looked like a sales table for Swarovski. He walked over to the small table and picked up crystal baby deer they had purchased on their first trip to Germany. "We are being ripped off. It is too cheap to be the real thing," she said. However, his innocent bewilderment at obtaining the crystal at such dirt-cheap prices made her smile and she quietly paid the money. And here they were today, the crystal, forty years, three children, and five grandchildren later, still in one piece—cheap or not.

Nita had embroidered a special tablecloth for the table— "Crystal Collection, N.S." "Now it can belong to both of us— Nita Singh and Nitin Singh," she joked.

He put the crystal back onto the table and made his way to the kitchen.

The night in the ER had drained him. He hated the sight and smell of hospitals. She had teased him, "Nitin, no one likes hospitals. It's not like people say, 'Oh I am not doing anything on Friday, do you want to go to GW Hospital?'"

A lingering lemony aroma of the curry leaves she had been sautéing last night embraced the house. She had been cooking just before she passed out.

Their youngest entered the house quietly behind him.

Nitin called out to him to be sure to take his shoes off.

They were good kids, more than what any parent could ask for. The twins in Texas were both physicians. The baby—gosh, he was twenty-seven—was part of a drama troupe. All grown up, all settled in their own realities. Yet he worried about them constantly. Nita had been able to cut the cord a lot better. Truth be told, he knew she was the practical one in their relationship. "Our parents, our kids, our siblings," she would joke, "they will all go about their own lives. Only you and I will be left, an old woman and her old man."

The harsh ringing of the phone brought his thoughts rudely back to the present. He walked to the phone, a high-tech toy he liked. Wireless with three receivers. But we are only two she insisted, why do we need three phones? The phone is so cool, was the rehearsed response. And so they had three phones. The ringing pierced the quiet of the house, the ID said "Out of Area." Nitin answered it. A sales drive for a local police charity. He politely declined. She would be upset with him. She always gave to the local charity. It rang again and this time he did not answer. His youngest answered it.

Nitin's attention was diverted to the notes tacked on the wall by the phone—"Call me when you get home, Nita." She had left him a note to call her. She never emailed him or texted him. She did that only with the kids once they left the house. With him, she always left him notes: buy milk/ where is my phone/ where is your phone/ what time is our dinner date/ do you want to see a movie/ I am off to the movies with the girls/ call me when you get home. Call her. Where could he call her now? He touched the note. Her essence emanated from each part of this house.

Nitin left the kitchen and continued walking toward their bedroom. That was the best thing he had done, she said—to have the bedroom on the main floor. She hated stairs. They are the devil on my knees, she complained. Each tired step brought him closer to the room. He turned the light on and then turned to her dressing table and stared blankly at the ornate mirror. This one was her choice, the mirror with its beautiful carved frame and golden peacock crown. He rarely interfered in decorating decisions.

Nitin ran his fingers across brightly colored bangles on the bangle stand. She purchased a dozen each year on their anniversary. Forty dozen bangles, a few broken or missing, hung merrily on the rods. Gorgeous bright colors, some studded with stones, and then there was her favorite, the ones with the tiny red bells attached. She bought those the year her first grandson was born. He had teased her a lot that day. These bangles are meant for sixteen-year-olds, he had said, and she shot him a cold stare. His fingers stopped intermittently at individual bangles, each one of them reminding him of her youth, their marriage, and their life. Some were from India— the stone-studded ones were from Hanuman Mandir, her favorite temple. The purple ones with rice pearls from Chandni Chowk in the back streets of old Delhi. Ah, the blue ones, that matched the sari he had brought for her from Dubai when he had won his big contract. The baby blue ones, that he told her to wear at least once a month for they reminded him of his successes, their successes. She loved wearing white, often accessorizing with belts, brooches, earrings, scarves of vivid colors. Her actions were as vivid as her accessories—she expressively waved her hands about when she talked, causing her signature glass bangles to jingle merrily.

The *mangalsutra*, the gold and black beads that signified marriage, should have been in its proper place. She usually placed it in its home—a printed silk bag, a gift from her long-departed mother-in-law. In Nitin's family, the tradition of a mangalsutra did not exist but Nita had insisted on one and her mother-in-law had rushed out to buy one. It signified for Nitin forty years of love and passion, of warmth and friendship, of closeness like no other. But today it lay carelessly strewn on the silver tray right beside the box of *sindoor*, the vermillion powder, the vermillion promise that they would be together in this lifetime and seven more.

The sindoor made his mind wander to their wedding day. The first time he applied sindoor, the vermillion powder of matrimony, in the part of her hair, he also proceeded to spill most of it on her nose. The wedding pictures showed her nose as red as a tomato as her sisters tried to rub the color away. It made him laugh. His memory may be poor but he remembered that as if it was yesterday.

She knew his memory was his weakness and would tease him about it every chance she got. For instance, for the life of him he could not remember when he first met her. They had been college sweethearts, but at what exact time did he first see her or where or with whom? He could not remember. He did remember the wedding, he often told her. "See I clearly remember the day I made your nose so red," he would laugh. And thank the Lord for that, she would respond and roll her eyes in pretend mockery. He suspected that she did not quite remember the first meeting either but was just better at pretending than he was.

Some memories were clearer than others, like the day she came home from work and declared they needed therapy since all her friends were having it. What in God's name for, he asked—they loved each other, did not fight or hate each other's guts, what in God's name for did they need therapy. She muttered, "We are so dull and boring. We are too normal. Maybe there is something wrong with us." That was Nita. Loving, charming, and so naïve, even at fifty-plus.

Nitin stared at his image in the mirror. When did he get so old? The wrinkles, the worry lines, and the gray hair? She said he looked sophisticated with his graying hair.

Old, he thought. *Now I just look old.*

His eyes wandered around their room, stopping to admire the large, engraved wooden box on the table. This sandalwood box held the most precious thing in the house: love letters from her to him. Decades of love, with its highs and lows, captured on her favorite pink pastel sheets. He saved them all in the box. In a way, he felt sorry for his kids, they would never be able to enjoy this kind of treasure; in this day of emails, he wondered what his kids would store.

He headed for the shower.

The hot water seemed understanding, washing away the night from hell, a night like no other. He reached for the soap and stopped. She had placed a new bar last week, chiding him for using slivers and not bothering to replace the soap. She was everywhere.

He toweled off. As he dressed in a simple white shirt and dark pants, he heard the kids in the living room. He smelled incense. Jasmine incense, her favorite. He smiled at his children's thoughtfulness, he was happy they had remembered their mother's choice.

He headed toward her table.

He picked up her hairbrush, the blue bangles, and the mangalsutra, and began to walk to the door.

He had forgotten something.

The sindoor.

He clumsily dropped the vermillion box while picking it up. The vermillion powder scattered all over the white carpet as though it too wept at the day. He tried to rub it off the carpet, the color became deeper. With a defeated sigh, he closed the lid on the small box and carried what was left in it.

His hand trembled as he walked into the living room.

He looked peaceful and quiet.

The room echoed his demeanor.

He felt sad as he looked at his son. The kids were home for a reunion, having arrived three days ago, not realizing it was the last time they would all be together.

A Hindu priest at the hospital had come to give her blessings. "Your wife … she is still a married woman, you must head home and bring the mangalsutra and the sindoor as soon as possible," he had advised.

Nitin did not want to leave the hospital but the kids insisted he go home for a few minutes. The kids, all grown up now, telling the parents what to do. One of the kids had accompanied him home to pick up the needful items requested by the priest.

Ah the kids, their kids. Not so little anymore, he thought.

Nita had worked like a maniac on her doctorate, he recalled, and gave it up in a heartbeat when they heard the first heartbeat of their twins. He wanted her to be home with them. It was an unspoken bond, he never asked her to quit. She never asked not to. She returned to complete her doctorate after the children started school.

"I have showered and now I am ready. Let's go to the hospital. I know she needs me," he told his son.

Today she was not their mother, not the grandmother of their kids, or the daughter of her parents Today she was simply his wife, his bride, his love.

She lay quietly on the cold metal bed.

She was as beautiful as the day they wed. Perhaps more. Becoming a mother and then a grandmother had added to her charm. He combed her hair with her hairbrush. Long and lustrous, it had been the envy of her sisters. Next came the bangles. They slipped on easily. She had a tiny wrist and as he had often remarked, painter's fingers, long and dainty.

He struggled with the mangalsutra, the necklace. His glasses? He could not see too well anymore. He stared helplessly at his son. The boy came over and unhooked the necklace and helped his dad place it around his mother's neck. She looked just like a new bride again. Almost.

The main mark of being a married woman was yet to be added.

The sindoor, the vermillion powder, was still needed. He opened the box, gently this time to ensure he would not spill it again on her nose. Using his index finger and his thumb, he pinched a bit of the red powder and placed in the part of her hair. Starting from the end of the part all the way to the front, in as much of a straight line as his trembling hands could afford to do. You always do it backwards, she would complain, it's front to back for the sindoor. A lesson he had still not learnt.

He reached the top of her forehead. His thumb imprinted a small dot on the middle of her forehead with the remaining powder.

Now she looked like a bride again.

Nita had been home last night cooking, then the fainting spell, the ER all night, the morgue in the morning, and now, now he had dressed her like his bride, again.

Quietly, the oldest moved the white sheet that had been covering the rest of her body to now cover her head—a sign of respect for the dead.

The Run

Anamika sat at the edge of the bathtub in her small apartment and began to weep. The lilac bathroom with its shimmering shower curtain, once alluring, seemed ghastly and psychedelic. The room began to spin and spin, out of control. She steadied herself. The sink, she needed to reach the sink. She staggered over and threw up. She had been back for a few hours now after being interrogated all morning by the police. They asked all kinds of questions about her past, about her present, about yesterday. They had her replay the scene over and over and over again. It was like dying a gruesome death many times over.

No detail was too small, they said, try and remember. *Sights, smells, people, who was there? What were they wearing? How long did you stay? Why did you leave her? Who else was there in the store? What were they wearing? Why did you go to the store? What did you and the lady at the counter talk about? Would anyone want to hurt you? Who are your enemies? How long were you standing in the store?*

After grueling hours at the station, the detectives then accompanied her back to the apartment. Her phones now had tracers. They went over each room with a fine-tooth comb looking for clues, signs that could give them a lead as to what happened the previous day. As they left, one of the officers approached her. "Ma'am, please don't leave town. We need you here."

They had no suspects except her, she figured. Yes, she was their prime suspect.

She threw up again and clutched at her stomach.

The stench overwhelmed her.

She threw up again; nothing came out. Her stomach was empty.

The situation seemed surreal: this is what happens to other people, not to regular, normal people. She held on and steadied herself. The vomiting sensation came back.

The phone was ringing. She ran out of the bathroom to answer it. Stumbling, anxious—perhaps it was the cops.

"Hi, Mom. No, no, they have not found her. Yes, I am so worried. No, you don't have to come over. Thank you for your call. Yes, I will call you the minute I hear anything, I promise." She hung up the phone.

Her parents had moved to Dubai when she turned seventeen. "This US life is not suiting us, we have to go somewhere else," her father said one morning, and her mother demurely followed him back. They ran a shoe store in Dubai and asked her several times to move back with them. She resisted—her life, or whatever was left of it, was here.

Anxiety forced her to do what she knew best: it was time for a run. She wanted to run and yet, she could not leave the house. What if the phone rang? But, she reasoned, she would have her cell phone with her.

The door bell rang and Anamika rushed toward the door, wondering if the cops had found something. She saw Rachel Dickson standing there, holding an envelope. "This came to me again, dear. It is for you. Is there any news?"

Anamika took the envelope and shook her head.

Ms. Dickson followed Anamika inside and closed the door behind her.

Rachel Dickson had always been a spot of sunshine in Anamika's lonely existence before Maya was born. Ms. Dickson, in her signature peach cotton nightgowns that barely reached down to her knees and a small white bun on her head, always greeted Anamika with a smile. At eighty-four, the old lady seemed to be shriveling away; she lived alone and never seemed to have any visitors. Yet she had always managed to smile, be personable.

Anamika felt a kinship toward the old woman, often wondering if that was to be her fate as well—alone at eighty.

As Anamika turned and walked over to her wrought-iron breakfast table to drop off the envelope that Ms. Dickson had bought her, she stared at her name on the envelope— Anamika. Her mother named her after a lovely, talented Indian actress's onscreen name: Anamika. The name translated meant – someone who has no name, no identity. Sadly, Anamika's relationship to the actress for whom she was named stopped at the name. Unlike the movie star, she did not consider herself a beauty. Her eyes were too close together; her nose, set off by a tiny diamond nose ring, was still too stumpy; and at five feet, she felt too short. She was the one no one remembered at dinner parties. She never offended anyone, but in truth felt that she never impressed anyone, either … one of a million.

There was no winning the name game for Anamika Singh.

Her mother truly loved Bollywood movies—the glitter, the glamour, the stars, the starlets, their hair, their shoes, their clothes, their makeup, and the outward beauty of it all. Each week her mother would order clothes for herself to match the new Bollywood styles, buy jewelry to keep up with the onscreen twenty-somethings' new looks, and even regale her friends with stories of her "inside" connections to the Bollywood superstars.

"Yes, yes. I know Rekha. She is a superstar but she is related to my dear friend. I have met her once; she really is beautiful. I even asked her for makeup tips and she told me how to apply lipstick." Each time her mother told the tale, the advice would change from lipstick to mascara to blush. She had indeed met Rekha, for all of thirty seconds at some movie premiere. She did not see the harm in adding a few details, which of course Rekha would have surely shared with her had they had the time together.

Anamika hated her name.

"A rose by any name," her father would say. It was not a solace.

"Come on, Dad. You know our names define who we are, regardless of that rose saying. What was Mom thinking?" she often said.

"Well, part of the problem is that your mother does not think," was his standard response.

At least she had made one contribution, one good deed that made her feel less guilty about occupying a place on Earth. Don't they say that some people are born to just plant a tree and others to reap the fruits? Perhaps that was it—that was the reason for her birth—to give birth to this loving child.

Her baby, gone for now. She needed to run.

"Ms. Dickson, would you stay here for a little bit? In case someone calls? I just need to run. I need to do something. I will take my cell phone with me," Anamika pleaded.

"Of course, child, I am here. I will call you the minute anyone calls. You go. Go and get some of this anxiety out."

Running helped Anamika clear her head, and right now she needed to think clearly. To try and remember more details so that she could help the cops to help herself. She needed to help, to do something, anything. Splashing cold water on her face, she stared at her image in the mirror. Dark circles, drawn cheeks, red eyes. *That is what terror looks like*, she thought.

She looked away, wiped her face, said a quick goodbye to Ms. Dickson, who had turned on the news, and headed to the tiny foyer of her apartment.

She reached for her favorite running shoes in their regular spot by the entry door. She loved these gorgeous shoes—women's Nike Air Max 360.

Her mother had rolled her eyes when she heard the price. "You bought shoes for $150? You could have bought yourself a nice dress or some makeup. Such a complete and total waste of money. You really need to learn to take care of your looks instead of wearing these boy shoes. You are a girl, not a boy. When will you realize that?"

For Anamika, it had been money well spent. She loved to run, free, unchained. Running provided a solace like nothing else. She owned six pair of shoes, five of which were running shoes and one a pair of grandmother pumps for the office. Slipping on her Nikes, she turned around and surveyed the apartment. The tiny white bassinet that sat in the middle of the room, surrounded by her sterile black and white furniture, was the essence of this room. Not just the room, the whole apartment. No, not just the apartment, it was the essence of her soul. The sight of the empty bassinet brought the pain back. The tears came back. What if they never found the baby? What would happen?

Her baby, her tiny beautiful helpless little baby, had been missing for over twenty-four hours now.

"It's critical we find her soon. The first few hours are critical. The possibility of finding her after that is … well …," some cop had told her.

The cops were being difficult, tough to be kind, or so one of them told her. The chances of finding a stolen baby were really minuscule and she needed to be prepared. She listened to them, trying to take it all in, to somehow get their words to sink in and make sense. They told her this, repeatedly as they questioned her. After the first four hours, the rest was a blur.

"Anamika, be sure to take your cell phone," Ms. Dickson called out to her as she shut the door. Anamika checked her waistband—the phone was there, hooked at her side.

During Anamika's pregnancy, Ms. Dickson was heaven-sent. She would show up just at dinner time each evening, holding a tray with colorful salads of spinach, oranges, blueberries, strawberries, and almonds. Then there would be a casserole or a piece of grilled fish or pasta with meatballs and even a dessert.

"Eat this for dinner. I know you must be hungry. You work too hard. Put your feet up, Anamika. You need to rest your body. How will this baby grow? When I had my kids, I would eat at least two bowls of pasta for dinner each night along with milk and at least a handful of almonds. That is why my sons were born at nine pounds. Big boys they were. They still are. Now, what else will you eat, child? No, no, this is not enough, how about some bread?" And she would literally run back to her apartment and reappear with rolls and butter. Her angelic presence was a balm to Anamika's raw nerves and inexperience with being pregnant.

"Women have been having babies forever, you are certainly not the first and you will not be the last, you will be fine, I know, I promise you, you will be fine. But see, see how your feet are swelling, it is because you don't rest them. Now finish your dinner and put your feet up. I will bring by a cup of chamomile tea around nine, it is soothing and you will sleep better. What will you eat for breakfast tomorrow? Not those sugary cereals—they are so bad for you. Or that horrible toast you like to eat. No, no, you need oatmeal with maple or yogurt with granola." Anamika adored Ms. Dickson's rhetorical monologues.

Most of the nine months passed with the same ritual.

Ms. Dickson loved to pamper her, and began to knit booties for the baby. "See, we will make these yellow booties so it will not matter if it is a girl or a boy. I made red ones and pink ones for my boys, no one cared about the colors back then. No, not so now. Now everyone wants blue or pink. I don't understand. Why does it matter? It really should not. My boys wore pink booties and they turned out fine. One even played college ball. Do you like yellow or should I make them green? I will just make them yellow. Yes, it is such a pretty color."

They went together for one of Anamika's ultrasounds, a technology that Ms. Dickson had complained all the way was not a good thing for the baby. But after seeing the little baby on the screen, the heart beating rhythmically and the tiny fingers almost reaching out, Ms. Dickson had begun to cry.

"I did not have this with my boys. I cannot believe it. It is such a miracle," she had then proceeded to hug a very startled ultrasound technician and ask, "Why is so dark in there? Can you not add some light so we can see the child's face? It all appears like a hazy movie, and that too in black and white? Can you not add color to this?"

Toward the end of the nine months, Anamika had called on her many evenings just to come by when it seemed the labor pains were starting. Ms. Dickson was a lifesaver, especially since her parents weren't there and the one-night-stand father of the baby had no idea that the baby even existed.

Anamika loved Ms. Dickson's nonstop chatter with Maya, the endless advice sessions, and the tiny little lemon-glazed bear-shaped cookies that Ms. Dickson often baked for her.

"I am off, Ms. Dickson, please call me if anything happens, I have my phone," Anamika said as she closed the door to her apartment. She had been to the site where Maya was last seen at least four times. Nothing, she could find no clue, no sign, nothing. She tried to remember the incident in detail to see if she could figure out anything. It was all a blur. Now, she debated staying home and waiting versus running. The run won out.

Anamika usually hated carrying anything when she ran except a few dollars tucked inside her socks. On her return, she would just punch in a code on the keypad at the main door to get in.

"What a smart feature," her mother said when Anamika first brought her parents over to show off her first apartment.

All was well until they reached the hallway to the apartment. Although it was clean, it smelled of stale smoke and rancid takeout. Her father could not stand it. "This place is a dump. How can you stay here? What will my friends say? This is what happens when you drop out of college. You live like a pig. I just don't understand you children. We give you everything. We sacrifice our life for you and this is what we get in return." He then pinched his nose to block off the offending odors, turned right around, and left. He never returned. Her mother handed her an envelope and said, "This is your housewarming gift. Don't tell your father," and then turned around and left.

That had been nearly a year and a half ago.

The envelope her mother gave her had contained a checkbook. She had opened an account for her with twenty thousand dollars. There was also a small note, "I love you. Please let me know if you need more. I will transfer money each month into this account." Her mother's kind gentleness tugged at her heart. She fought her immediate reaction, "Mom, I can take care of myself. I don't need this cash." She knew her mother would be heartbroken if she returned the money. She kept the checkbook but never withdrew any money from it until Maya was born. Then she transferred the account to Maya's name. Her mother was thrilled. "I am so proud of you, Anamika. I am a blessed woman."

Anamika raised her hand to press the down button on the elevator. Before she could press the button, the door opened and a bald young man standing inside smiled at her, signaling her to get in. She managed a smile. "Nice to see you, Kirk."

"Going for a run? You don't look so good. Any news on the baby? The cops were around asking questions," asked Kirk, showing his talent for asking the obvious.

"No, nothing yet … I am so, so worried," she responded.

"I am sorry. It will be fine. They will find her," he said.

How much can change in twenty-four hours.

Yesterday morning, they were both in the elevator at the same time and the discussion had been about his job search. "Ah, my search—it is going nowhere fast. I interviewed at the State Department last week and they said to come back in two weeks. So now instead of twiddling my thumbs, I am going to work at a small landscaping company, clearing out trees," he replied.

And today, they were discussing her missing baby.

Kirk was nineteen or twenty and had moved in around the same time she had. He seemed like a regular, normal kid. He seemed extra careful and extra polite all the time, going out of his way to hold the door for her, calling on her when he made his grocery store runs to see if she needed milk. It was one of those relationships formed out of a mutual desire to connect with another human being as if to say "Look at me, damn it. I am alive. I have a life. I buy milk."

Kirk interrupted her thoughts.

"Your eyes are so red and swollen. You have been crying? Please don't worry—I saw the Amber alert on TV last night. Don't worry, they will find her. Cops here are really good. They have been all over the building questioning people. They will find her. I am sure." She nodded gently, desperately trying to share his faith in the cops. He held the elevator for her as it opened. She waved goodbye as he stepped out and turned toward the laundry room on the main floor of the building.

As she stepped outside the building, onto the concrete driveway, she shivered in her thin white cotton t-shirt. Winter was technically more than three months away, but the cold breeze and falling leaves told a different story. There were two cops outside, talking to people. They nodded as they saw her and she nodded back. Kirk was right—at least they were doing their job.

She checked her phone. Nothing. She hooked her phone back onto her waistband.

Anamika stretched for a few minutes and then began to walk, steady at first, and then faster. As her body got into the rhythm, her mind wandered—the nightmare of the day past began to replay in her mind. A tip from a woman's magazine she had read earlier that week buzzed in her head—say a prayer as you run to steady your mind.

Could a prayer bring the baby back? She had never prayed before. How exactly did one pray?

It all happened so suddenly. She, her friend Mita, and Mita's on-again, off-again boyfriend, Kit, were at their favorite Tako Take-Out, a red-walled, cozy sushi restaurant at the corner of Maple and Elder Streets in the charming town of Vienna. Kit, who always reminded Anamika of a young Richard Gere, had given Mita a ride to the restaurant. "I just wanted to see the babe," he said and picked Maya up and out of her car seat. "You are going to be such a heartbreaker, look at those big, brown eyes. Now give me a big kiss," he planted a big, sloppy kiss on Maya's cheek and she in turn obliged him with one of her glittering smiles. "Have a good lunch, ladies. I am off," and he was gone.

"How can you not fall in love with him, Mita? Good God, he is sooo gorgeous," Anamika often teased her friend. Kit was usually so shy; it was nice to see him show so much emotion with Maya.

The restaurant was quiet, a small wall-mounted water fountain providing a soothing melody, and three-month-old Maya slept through most of the lunch. Mita constantly fussed over the tiny, beautiful infant.

"Isn't she beautiful? She takes after her mother," Mita told Anamika repeatedly.

"I look like her nanny, not her mother! She does not resemble me at all, I guess thankfully so."

Mita just laughed. She was still recovering from a cold and tried to keep a safe distance from the baby. She felt a flu coming on.

Anamika and Mita had always been together in their search for perfection. As teenagers, their favorite activity was the weekly jaunts to the mall to admire the wafer-thin girls in their short skirts, heels, and shimmering blond hair. Sometimes they would stand outside Victoria's Secret and marvel at the figures of the mannequins in black lace. Other times they would go through *People* magazine together at their local Borders, marking up all they would have done when they had the money—the nose, the boob job, the lipo. They never did get the surgeries but each found other outlets. Anamika began to run and Mita found men. Their friendship had endured a lot—gossip, dysfunctional family members, and overzealous boyfriends asking for threesomes. Finally, they both admitted, they had found a happy place with Maya and Kit.

"We are ready for the check," Anamika said to their dark haired Asian waiter as he rushed past them.

After lunch, Mita, feeling dizzy, had called Kit and left to go home. Anamika with a still-sleeping Maya had strolled into the busy India Spice World grocery store next door.

Anamika placed the car seat holding Maya on the floor, next to the crowded, overflowing and somewhat dusty shelves housing the latest Indian movies, and began to look at the new titles to see if she liked anything. She placed her handbag right next to the car seat.

A young Japanese girl with tight jeans and a pink t-shirt approached her. "Anamika! Hi!"

Anamika turned to see who it was.

"Lisa! What are you doing here?" she responded to her much younger friend, who worked at a clothing store in Georgetown.

"I am here with my mom, we are buying a present for our Indian neighbor who is having some sort of baby shower. I found out that this store sells Indian costume jewelry so we thought she would like that. Is that Maya?"

Anamika nodded and Lisa and her mother cooed and coddled the baby for a moment. "She is so cute. How old is she now?"

"Almost three months!"

Lisa then said a formal goodbye and turned her attention to her mother, who was already talking to a young Indian lady at the counter to finish paying for all their purchases.

"See you later, Anamika, on one of your runs!" Lisa waved goodbye.

Anamika waved to her and then turned back to talk to the lady at the counter about renting some movies. The young woman told her to wait for a few minutes as she finished with a customer on the phone.

As she waited, Anamika turned to look at the spice racks on the other side of the store.

"Okay, I am ready now," the lady at the movie counter called out to Anamika.

Anamika turned to the counter to pick out the movies.

"I will take those three. How much?" she said and looked down to get her purse that she had placed right next to Maya's car seat.

It was gone. The seat, the baby, all gone.

And so mundanely did the nightmare begin.

It seemed like five minutes ago.

It seemed like a lifetime ago.

And now here she was running in the middle of Georgetown to save herself from her own thoughts. Anamika began to run, fast, a life-saving run. Fast, faster, faster. Suddenly she was at a light, right in the middle of M street. A red sports car screeched to a halt right in front of her.

"What the fuck are you doing? Watch where you're going, lady!" the driver yelled through the open car window as he slammed his brakes. She muttered an apology. He flipped her and continued on. She knew what he must be thinking: *Damn immigrants, can't see the road.* She slowed down her pace and began to walk. The wind was stronger, colder; she pulled her t-shirt closer as she tried to huddle from the relentless chill.

She checked her phone. There was a text from Mita asking if there was any news. Nothing else.

Tears began streaming down her cheeks as the nightmare unfolded in her mind again.

"Maya, Maya, where are you? Where is my baby? She was right here. Did you see her? ... Hey mister, did you see a baby here? She was right here. Did you see her?" she had begun to scream uncontrollably as she rushed to each person in the Indian store.

Everyone shook his or her head; no one seemed to know what happened or how the baby vanished. The lady at the counter ran up and opened the front door to look outside,

"No one is here. I don't see anyone with a baby! Somebody call the police, call 911."

For a minute Anamika thought it was someone's idea of a joke. Who would take a tiny baby? It all seemed so unreal. Maya was just here, less than five minutes ago; she was here in her car seat, sleeping contently.

Anamika began to shake, cry and scream all at the same time. "What am I going to do? Oh, my God. My baby. How could I have left her there? Who would take her? Oh my God, oh my God. She has to be here. Oh God...." She took out her cell phone and called 911. The lady at the counter called 911, too.

Anamika then called Mita and left a panicked message. "Maya is ... Maya is gone. She is missing. Can you come here? I am here at the India Spice World on Maple, can you please get here as fast as possible. She was here a minute ago and, and, and, I don't know what happened, Mita, can you please come. I don't know what to do."

The cops arrived within three minutes of the 911 call and began to question everyone in the store. The customers who had been very cooperative initially were beginning to get antsy.

"I already told you, I did not see anyone. Why would someone leave the baby and not pay attention? What kind of a parent does that?" The comments came at Anamika from all sides.

"Get all contact information before letting them go," some cop was saying.

More voices, all melding together. "Find out if they have security cameras here." "Get the license plates of all the cars parked outside."

"Ms. Singh, Ms. Singh, where did you place the car seat? How long was the baby alone? What was she wearing? Do you have a recent picture? You will need to come to the station with us."

The cold breeze on M street seemed to get stronger and Anamika began to feel even her walking pace slow down even more. The walk died into a drag. It was unlike her; she could normally finish this entire run in less than thirty minutes and today she could barely walk. Running had saved her many times—after she first told her therapist about the incidents with her classmates hating her and calling her names, she had run. After kids had thrown dog feces at her and called her a fat cat, she had run. A run had saved her each time. It cleared her head and gave her perspective.

Not today.

The run seemed to be losing its power.

She checked her phone again. Then called Ms. Dickson. There was no update.

It was getting colder; the sun was setting beyond the maze of buildings.

Streams of people poured through the street—dressed in the newest fashions, their feet nestled in the latest leather sling-backs and high heels. Faceless, nameless crowds desperately trying to look like they belong. It was an interesting contrast, the latest fashions being paraded outside some of DC's oldest buildings.

"Everyone on M street is thinner, taller, blonder, more beautiful, and of course more successful. I don't know why you go there. It is depressing," Mita would say. Oddly, in this most stylish district in Washington, DC, Anamika felt right at home. No one had the time to look at her. They were all lost in their own worlds.

The tip from the woman's magazine on prayer buzzed in her mind again.

Perhaps she could just pray for help, she wondered as she watched the stream of people flow by.

She had never prayed, her mother had never prayed, never showed her how to pray. Her father was never particularly religious and never went back to any form of prayer.

There had never been any spiritual anchor in her parent's 6,500-square-foot home in McLean. It was filled with things—brass statues, Lladro sculptures, the finest Austrian crystal, raw silk curtains, and outrageously expensive Italian furniture. As a family, their entire lives revolved around her father's quirks—if he wanted to go shopping, they went shopping. If he decided that they had to go to, say, Madagascar for the summer, they went. He thrived on all that glittered—the king of 800-thread-count sheets. He was famous for breaking plates, slamming doors, and even leaving the house for days. Her best times with her mother were when her father would leave town. They would head out for pizza at Ledo's down the street. Mom would tell jokes, buy them large sodas, even drive to McDonalds for hot fudge sundaes. At night they would watch scary movies together and her mother would imitate the skull snatcher/bone crusher/ eye-ball collector or whoever was the central villain in the movie and give Anamika more playful scares. When her father would return, things would go back to being "plastic."

Then he went to Dubai one day and decided that it was better there than here and moved within three months.

Her mother rarely, if ever, reacted to her father but even she had slightly protested, "Our entire life is here, how can we just leave?" He never bothered to answer.

Anamika knew that her mother's heart was broken. Her mother would have made someone such a loving wife. She recalled with guilt the nights she would spend wishing that her mother would run away or find someone new. She would scan the personals on the Internet and have a list of men ready. She would pick the ones with gentle eyes, the ones who looked kind and could give her mother the love she so severely lacked. Her list kept getting updated. Just in case. That day, of course, never arrived. Anamika grew up, and her mother grew old. Her parent's relationship seemed to have more regrets than tenderness. They all coexisted, even peacefully at times, but mostly in spite of each other. She had called and left them a message about Maya and had gotten a call back immediately. Her mother had assured her that they would help pay any ransom, anything at all.

Anamika began to run faster, faster, faster, until all the thoughts left her head.

"What's your rush, it's all still gonna be there," a young man sitting in the middle of the bridge chided her. She turned to look at him, tripped and fell on her face, splitting her lip. Blood began dripping down her chin. He got up and offered her a hand. She took it and stared at his eyes. He was ruggedly handsome, with rumpled, ripped clothing and really bad body odor; clearly he was living on the streets. She had seen and spoken him every day for the past two months. Initially, she had wondered—*What is a good-looking young man like this doing on the streets?*—as though being good-looking were a license to having a good life.

"It's me, Eddie," he offered with eyes averted. "Don't you remember? You gave me a twenty last week." She was used to him reintroducing himself each time she met him.

"Yes, of course I do. How are you? Did you eat something?" She tried to look him in the eye. He never looked at her directly, always kept his gaze directed toward the pavement.

He smiled, "Yes, I had a full meal, three times! Thank you."

"How do you feel today, Eddie?" she asked.

He smiled. "My friends, they back, Ms. Ana, they are back. They went away and now they are back. I don't know why. I say to them to go away—see I even pulled my hair out—because they come from here, here in the center of my brain. Tell them to leave me alone Ms. Ana, tell them to go away," he began to weep.

She sat down next to him and gave him a gentle hug. His "friends," as he often called them, were imaginary beings she had seen him speaking to many times. She had offered to take him to a clinic but he refused. She reached into her sock and pulled out a twenty.

"Keep this, Eddie, eat something."

He smiled at her. "The jacket you gave me keeps me so warm, Ms. Ana. It is so cold out here. The jacket is so warm. I am so cold at night."

"Tomorrow, I will bring you some more clothes but right now I have to go."

He held onto her hand as she stood up to continue her run.

She tugged her hand.

He let her hand go and she ran, a ship-wrecked soul, desperately looking to the horizon for some relief, a touch of hope, a hint of relief but finding nothing but despair and hopelessness.

Faster and faster. The thoughts pulsated through her body, resonating with each step, thumping at her temples, pushing through each pore of her body, each step tormenting her with more despair.

Was it possible to run away from yourself? There was only one way to find out.

She ran and ran until she could run no more and collapsed on the ground unable to move.

A dog walker gently helped lift her up off the pavement and shook his head. "You are bleeding, lady. Are you okay? Be careful, you will hurt yourself." She wanted to thank him but stopped. He seemed wafer thin, like a ghost almost. He smiled weakly as she opened her mouth, and then turned around and kept on walking.

She began to walk back toward her apartment. The sky was darker, the wind was colder. Her t-shirt, now bloodstained, offered no comfort or warmth.

There was so much noise in her head. She tried to shut it out. Focus on something else, she thought. Her bloodstained shirt attracted uninvited glances and whispers. She ignored them and kept walking.

The cops were gone and the outside of her building was deserted.

Back in the warmth of her apartment, she saw that Ms. Dickson had fallen asleep in the armchair. The TV was still on. She turns it off.

Anamika first checked all her messages—nothing on the voicemail, nothing on the cell phone, no emails. Nothing. No news.

She walked over to the bathroom. It still smelled of vomit.

She ran the shower. The warm water gently flowing down her face, her belly, her legs and her feet, calmed her down. Her lip had swelled and throbbed.

She heard the phone and ran out of the shower, dripping wet. Maybe it was the detective. Maybe the cops. Maybe they found her and this nightmare was over.

It was Mita calling.

Anamika answered, "No, no news yet. We will find her. Don't worry. Please don't cry. We will find her. I am just drying off from a shower. I will call you later. Yes, I promise, I will call you as soon as I hear."

She thought of leaving a message for the baby's father. What was the point? He was married with a new life, he probably would consider this an imposition on his new life.

She wished the call had been from the police or the kidnapper. The cops told her that if it was a kidnapping, she would get a call within a few hours demanding a ransom. Anamika's bank balance could barely cover six months of basic expenses.

She just wanted her baby back, she would give anything.

She dropped to her knees near the phone and began to weep. Where was her baby? Still wet from the shower, she began to get the chills. Water dripped from her hair and a wet spot formed around her on the carpet, forcing her to get up and go back to the bathroom. She dried herself and put on a pair of pajamas.

She wandered into the kitchen and for the first time in well over twenty-four hours thought about food. She had learned to love the warmth of the stove by spending time with her mother. Watching her mother cook was a joy in itself. She was no gourmet chef or outstanding cook but she cooked with abandon, without recipes but with heart—a little of this and a little of that constituted her mom's style. When the dishes were finally served, it really did not matter what she had cooked. She served it with great gusto and style, making even omelets and toast seem like a connoisseur's delight.

Anamika would return from dinners at her parents very inspired to cook. It would last for a few days until of course the realities of being alone would gnaw at her heart, turning her away from her beloved stove and to fast-food joints. It was such a distressing waste: cooking for one. Half-used cans of soup, half-used onions, and containers of chicken curry that she swore kept filling up magically on their own—no matter how much she ate, there always seemed to be stuff left in it. She opened the fridge. The baby's bottles were stacked neatly, waiting. She picked one up, smelled it and then held it close to her heart. The bottle smelled of missing joy.

Suddenly, she felt famished.

She needed to eat something. Anything.

She decided on a no-fuss meal—scrambled eggs with green chiles and buttered toast. And tea. Yes, of course. It was a habit she acquired from her mother—any time of the day or night was teatime.

She prepared the eggs and toast and boiled the water for the tea for two. She would wake Ms. Dickson up to eat with her. The soothing fragrance of cardamom tea filled the atmosphere. The eggs, her favorite meal, just sat there on the pan. She picked up a spoon to eat them. Then put it down. How could she eat when Maya could be somewhere starving? Perhaps people were right, she was not a good mother. Here she was getting ready to wolf down a meal … while … …

The eggs and the toast stayed on the plate.

She poured herself a cup of tea and walked into her bedroom and turned on the TV. She had not seen the Amber alert Kirk had mentioned and wanted to see what they were saying on TV.

She quietly sipped her tea as the white noise of the television drowned out reality. The phone was quiet. She watched it, wanting it to ring. Two calls did come—Mita, checking in again, and her mom calling to see if she had heard anything. Anamika instinctively curled up into the folds of the couch and hugged the phone close to her heart ... checking for a dial tone every few minutes to make sure it was working correctly.

She looked around her room. She had only two pictures— one of her mother and one of Maya. There was another frame, a gift from someone at work, that still had the picture of a perfect, nameless model, just as it had been bought. The frame demanded just the right shot. She had none.

The files on the table beckoned her. She could work. Work always took her mind off of everything else. Her simple accounting job paid the bills. She opened her files and stared at the paper. The words seem to all run together, the numbers made no sense. Tears dripping on the paper smudged the invoices she was to review. The phone rang again. Eleven o'clock. She got up and checked caller ID. Mita. She suddenly felt drained and tired. "No, Mita, nothing yet. Yes, I promise to call you. You don't sound good. Are you okay? Okay ... bye."

She hung up the phone and put her head down on the table. Her tired eyes closed as the tears still flowed.

A noise startled her. She could hear beeps.

She opened her eyes. She had fallen asleep at the table, over her files. Again. The alarm was ringing in her room.

The living room clock showed 4:00 am. It was 4:00 am on September 7, now two whole days that Maya had been missing.

The poor baby, she worried that whoever took her would not know how to feed her, she needed to be burped after each feeding, and loved to nap without a blanket. She cried when she needed her mom or when she had a wet diaper. She fussed only when she had gas. Oh, what was going to happen?

Anamika felt it had just been her all this while with no one to observe her life; no one to witness her success or failure, with her mother just barely being able to flit in and out of her existence. Maya had changed her intentionless existence.

Suddenly she was wide awake. She got up and habitually stretched her back and then checked her phone again. Six calls from Mita and nothing else.

She checked in on Ms. Dickson, who was sleeping soundly on the armchair.

"I should have at least woken her up for dinner," Anamika thought and then went back to the table and reached for her journal. It provided her with comfort on many lonely nights and long, tedious days.

Her fingers traced the three *U*s inscribed on the cover. No one knew what they stood for, except her—the three *U*s that defined her.

She reread her first entry "The three *U*s. Ugly, unloved, and unwanted. Ugly I can deal with. Hey, it is the face the Universe gave me. Unloved. This is who I am. I have tried to be so much with so many people and ended up being nothing to anyone. Unwanted. This one is the hardest one of all. Being unwanted. When no one needs you. No one calls you. No one misses you. When you don't matter in anyone's life. That really is the hardest … being unwanted and feeling like a burden."

She flipped the journal pages. It opened to the entry she had made when she had discovered she was pregnant. "Pros and cons of having a baby alone. Cons—Children need a mother and a father figure. Pros—I can love this child like no one else. Cons—I am not rich. Pros—I make enough for a simple life." The list went on for pages. "Cons—I will need to add another U to the cover for "unattached single mother!"

The decision was simple. She knew in her heart she would keep her baby.

She remembered the morning well. She had placed a hand on her stomach, it felt like an alien gesture. "You are mine. You and I will be together forever. I never have to be alone again."

Even before she began to see an obstetrician, Anamika signed up to see a therapist again. Years of neglect that had all been shoved under the carpet came to a head. And she had never felt better. "I am bigger than this, I am not just an unworthy life, I am here for a reason,"—the entries in her journal began to show hope. Maya Singh was born on May 29. She had light brown hair in gentle curls.

The phone began to ring again. Anamika ran to answer it.

"Yes? Yes, this is Anamika Singh."

"Ms. Singh, I am calling from DC TV. Have you heard that there are unconfirmed reports that the police found the body of a young baby in the Potomac this morning? Is this your daughter? Have the police contacted you yet?"

The phone fell from her hands.

It was over. Just like that. It was over.

She stood there numb. Unable to move, to speak, to think. Her cell phone rang, and rang, and rang. She sat on the floor and stared at the ceiling.

The doorbell rang and Anamika stared at the door, unable to move.

Ms. Dickson got up and saw Anamika on the floor.

"What happened, child? Who is at the door? Did they find her?"

"Ms. Singh, this is the Detective Peters. Open the door please, Ms. Singh, please open the door." He began to bang on the door, "Ms. Singh?"

"Anamika, stay here. I will open the door."

Ms. Dickson walked to the door and opened the latch.

"I need to see Ms. Singh, I have news. You are…?"

"I heard, Detective, I heard, she's gone …," Anamika answered from inside the apartment. She was crying.

"What? She's gone? What happened?" Ms. Dickson began to cry.

"The reporter, he, he said they found a body …." her voice trailed off and she began to weep.

"What, what are you talking about? You both need to stop crying. LISTEN TO ME. STOP CRYING," the detective tried to get their attention by raising his voice.

They both stopped and stared at him.

"I came to take you to the hospital where she is being checked. Someone dumped her in a nearby trash heap and a guy walking his dog found her and took her to GW Medical

Center. She is fine," the detective said in his loudest voice to be heard over the wailing of the two women.

Could it be that her baby was okay?

Ms. Dickson helped her stand up.

"Let's get our baby home, Ms. Dickson, let's get her home," Anamika said.

Doubts

Geet met Nihad at a singles' dinner that her old friend Reena had hosted on the large patio of her charming house. The chemistry between her and Nihad was instant as they stood on the side of the patio, sipping Coke.

"I am Nihad Pandit. It is nice to meet you," said the well-built, light-eyed, olive-skinned young man. Geet prided herself on being able to place accents. "I am the reincarnation of Professor Higgins," she would joke. But she could not tell where he was from—he looked Asian but his accent seemed very different.

"Where are you from?" she casually inquired.

"Well, it is complicated. My father was from Kashmir. He went to college here in the US. He went to Syria for vacation one year and met my mother there. So I guess I am a Kashmiri Syrian American! Is that even an ethnicity? I guess I am the melting pot!"

"You are like me! My mom was Pakistani and Dad was a third-generation Indian living in Trinidad. I guess I am a melting pot, too! It is nice to meet you."

Reena offered him some wine.

"No thanks! I am fine with soda," he had said.

"You don't like wine?" Geet asked as Reena walked away.

"Well, it is a religion thing. I have never had a drink. It is against my religion."

"In this day and age? Are you Muslim? I mean, your last name … is that a Muslim name?" she asked, suddenly conscious of the lack of religion in her own life. Then added, "I hope I am not prying! I am just curious. Your last name sounds Hindu and I don't think it is against Hinduism to drink. Although I know very little about religions in general!"

"No, worries. It is an unusual name. I get the question a lot. My father was a Hindu and my mother is a Muslim. He married her against her parents' wishes. My mother named me Nihad, I think it means horses or heights or something in Arabic. When Dad died, I was two, my mother raised me on the Koran. It is the only religion she was familiar with," he said as he sipped his Coke. He smiled at her.

"Ah, that is so interesting. My parents were both Muslim, but nonpracticing. I don't think I have even seen a Koran, much less read one," Geet replied.

"Well, just so you know that is as exciting as it gets with me. The rest of my life, well, I am really very boring. I don't drink or smoke or, well, you know … no drugs, no fast cars or anything!" His smile was gentle. "Simple rules to live by and they actually keep life easier."

Were there people this simple left in the world?

"So now, it is my turn," he said with a beaming smile and fired off a list of questions:

"What do you like to do? Where did you grow up? Where did you go to school?"

"Ah, I am an adjunct professor at Georgetown. I live by myself. My parents died a few years ago in an accident and I have been alone since." She was a bit embarrassed at sharing so much with a total stranger.

Focusing all her attention on him, she asked, "Okay, that is it, now it is my turn—what is it that you do?"

"Oh, me? Nothing radical … I just started a consulting gig with a small company. I do some financial consulting—you know, helping people plan their estates and all that."

As he talked, she noticed a long, fresh scar in the center of his left palm.

"Ah, that," he smiled.

"My biggest vice—fire power! I love firecrackers. This one went off in my hand. Needed nearly twenty stitches and damn near gave my mother a heart attack." The scar was deep, fresh.

Geet loved that he had a casual air about him. He kept on talking and she kept on smiling and listening. The night ended when Reena threw them out at four in the morning, "Go home! How are you two still here? You haven't even had a single drink! Aren't you bored?"

Geet left in a trance. She really liked him. She liked him a lot. She did not believe in the whole "love at first sight thing" but today she was having second thoughts. Nihad, dressed in a casual cotton shirt and jeans, with dark, curly hair, was the ideal boy next door. She wondered if he felt the same. He had taken her number before he left and she wondered if he would call.

She only had to wait a few hours to find out.

At nine in the morning, the first flower delivery arrived with a note: "Dinner? With me and without wine?"

One dinner turned into two and then three and then four. They saw each other every night that week. On Friday, he told her he wanted to introduce her to his family.

"Your family? Aren't we moving rather fast?" Geet teased.

"In a normal relationship, yes, it would be fast. But in my world, this is step one in getting to know me. Besides, my mother knows I am seeing someone and has refused to let me back in the house until I bring you with me," Nihad said and laughed.

Despite her initial hesitation, Geet found that she loved meeting his family. His mother, Fatima, was raising eight kids. Nihad was the oldest and helped her around the house with the chores and the other kids. The kids were not related to either Nihad or Fatima. Fatima took them in as a foster parent—children of displaced lands and war-torn countries. She cared for them until the system knew what to do with them.

Geet began to love spending time with Fatima. Although Fatima ran a strict household with kids of many different temperaments, the house was always vibrant and brimming over with food, laughter, and noise. The kids were constantly running around, Fatima running behind them, and Nihad chasing them all down. They all sat together and ate from one single large plate, a custom Geet found endearing. They spoke different languages—there was a kid from Somalia, one from Darfur, two from Bangladesh and three Syrian girls—yet they all melded into Fatima's giving home. Fatima took them to school, enrolled them in soccer, taught them how to play the piano, and at night read to them from the Koran. The more time Geet spent there, the more she felt like she belonged.

"You are in love with his family, Geet, not with him," Reena said once. It took Geet by surprise. It was true that she adored Nihad but Reena's insight made her want to explore her relationship with Nihad a bit further.

And that seemed difficult because of Nihad's attitude towards the man–woman relationship. He refused to get intimate, even when she initiated the touch. Every other man she had met wanted to jump in bed and once that was done, to jump as far away from commitment as possible. They had been out on many dates and he never attempted to get physical. In fact, he insisted on a sexless relationship venturing only so far to kiss her, almost platonically, on her cheeks.

"Are you sure he isn't gay?" Reena asked one day as they shopped for new running shoes. There were a lot of reports in the *Washington Post* that week about American Muslims fronting a heterosexual relationship to hide the fact that they were gay. It said that some Muslim men posted proposals on a dating website to find partners who would marry them for a public front so that they could keep their family happy, but not expect any sex. "That is so damn ludicrous," Geet countered, but the comment hit her hard.

Could it be? Was he gay?

Was he using her as a front to hide his identity from his family? Or was it that Reena's comment about being in love with the family more than with him was true and that she had just not taken the time to really notice?

Geet began to spy on him to find out if he was indeed gay.

She noted he often had male friends over. They would go into his bedroom together and shut the door. They would stay locked in there for what seemed like hours on end. While she spent time with Fatima watching the kids, discussing food, movies, and politics, Nihad and his buddies would be in the room with the door closed. There were three in all and they always seemed to be together. Great, she thought, he is gay and into groups. That is what is wrong with him. She began to show up uninvited to his house. Fatima would always welcome her and invite her in and never seemed to mind that she never called before coming. In fact the more she came unannounced, the friendlier they seemed. Fatima said, "I am so glad you are not into the Western custom of making appointments to come over; back home, people would come over anytime of the day. Shows friendliness, like family, yes?"

Each visit filled her with more guilt. Nihad seemed truly happy to see her each time. It did not calculate. If he was really in there doing something, then why did he not get mad at her? Why was he so nice when she showed up? She began to formulate a plan. There was no way he really loved her. This was all a front and she was determined to find out the truth. What the hell was going on in there? The foursome now rarely went behind closed doors and had relocated into the main living room.

From that time on, each evening she went over, she would leave Fatima talking in the kitchen and move to the living room where she could hear Nihad and his friends. They spoke in Arabic and she could not understand anything.

A few weeks later it happened. She walked in on Nihad and his friends sitting on the floor poring over some papers. It was the first time they all stopped talking as soon as they saw her. She noticed on the floor there seemed to be architectural plans, blueprint-like drawings. The title read MALL, with some word preceding it that she could not see. "We are just researching something," he said when she asked.

"But what are you researching, Nihad?"

"You will see, one day the whole world will see what we can do! My friends and I are going to change the way America shops!" She tried all week to get him to say more and each time he brushed it off. "It is a secret. It will be so big, you will see. It will make us famous! I am not ready to share yet but soon, I promise."

Frustrated by his responses, later the next week, she went over to Reena's to relay the situation and get some advice.

"Oh, my God," her friend, high as a kite, countered.

"He is not a fucking fag, Geet. He is a goddamn terrorist. Change the way America shops? Geet, they are going to bomb a mall. Don't you get it … which mall is it … what the hell were they talking about? Did you not pick up any part of the conversation? Oh, my God!"

A terrorist? Could Reena be right? But he seemed so normal to Geet. Reena had a penchant for exaggeration but all the little pointers … the plans to the mall, how they had stopped talking when she entered the room. They did not want her to know. Geet began to panic. What the hell were these men doing? The more she and Reena talked that day, the more Reena tried to convince Geet that Nihad was about to attack the mall.

As Geet listened to Reena rattle on, she tried to reason with herself. He was a good man. Fatima was an amazing person. This was no terrorist household. Reena was wrong.

Geet decided to stop listening to Reena's nonsense and headed home.

She had just left Reena's house when her cell phone rang. Reena was barely coherent on the phone, "I just made the call Geet. I called the cops. Nihad will be behind bars soon." Geet dropped the phone. Shaking, she called Nihad but there was no answer. She hailed a cab and headed to Nihad's house.

There she witnessed a scene that would haunt her forever. A man was going to be labeled a terrorist and she had no idea if he was one or not. She stared in horror as the cops arrived along with black Suburbans filled with people in dark suits. She stood outside his house watching them all go in. After what seemed like hours they emerged with Nihad, not handcuffed, and drove off.

How could they just take him? How did they know what Reena said was true? It could not be. But, what if it was? No ... no, it could not be. Why on earth had they not checked things out before coming here?

She wanted to go up to the house.

She wanted to console Fatima. To say, "I am sorry. My friend thought your son was a traitor, a terrorist, she did this. She did not mean it. She is a good person. I am so sorry."

The door opened again and Fatima came out beating her chest and screaming loudly in Arabic. All Geet could make out were the words, "*Allah, Allah.*" Fatima's wailing attracted the neighbors and a few of them, whom Geet recognized as Fatima's friends, left their houses, and began walk toward her house. Geet turned around to see if she could flag another cab before Fatima spotted her. There was not a cab in sight and so she began to run to the Metro stop to go back home. She could not stand this.

She hated what she had done. Why had she trusted Reena? Why had she told Reena anything?

The next three days were quiet. Not a peep from Nihad or his family.

Geet barely slept, constantly concerned that someone would show up at her door and take her down for being a snitch. No such thing happened.

Then on the third night, two things happened. First, her phone rang and it was Nihad. She was afraid to answer the phone. He left a message. "Geet, I am so sorry I have not called. Did you talk to my mother? Have you heard? This is all so insane. Totally insane. Who would do this to me? My friends and I were planning to design and set up malls here like there are in Dubai. I cannot believe someone called the cops on us. I should be home later today. Call me." The phone fell from her hands as she stood there frozen in time. It all happened so fast.

Second—the cops came in to question her about him. She told them, she had seen the plans they had. Yes, they were planning to design and open a brand new-style mall. The cops were convinced and left her. "Someone made a complaint and we had to check it out. But there is not one piece of evidence that supports the complaint. Not one. But you know, these days, we have to check everything," one of the detectives told her as he was leaving.

Geet could not summon up the nerve to call Nihad back. She did not know how to face him. Her stupidity had caused him so much pain. She was so ashamed.

He kept calling her, stopping by, emailing, IMing. Finally, he gave up. His final email: "I cannot believe that you believe all the crap they are saying about me. I thought we loved each other, Geet. Why don't you ever call me back?"

Some why's are better left unanswered.

A month passed and Geet was miserable. She missed him so much. She missed Fatima. She missed the kids. She decided to go and tell them everything and to apologize. She felt that perhaps they would forgive her stupidity.

She woke up that morning, anxious and excited. She was going to go to his house. She turned her computer on. She would send him an email to let him know she was coming.

There was an email from Reena with the subject line: Nihad hurt.

Reena had sent Geet a tiny item from the *Washington Post* about a Middle Eastern man, Nihad Pandit, who went into a butcher shop in Alexandria and someone had tried to cut off his right arm. Authorities would not confirm if he had done it to himself or if someone had done it to him. Someone interviewed for the piece suggested it was done by a man angry that Islam was given a bad name by the likes of Nihad planning terrorist attacks against innocent people.

Geet shut down her computer and began to cry.

Dear John

I knew when I sat in John's Dodge Dart that day, with Alice Cooper blasting on the radio, that we could never go back home again. Never, ever. We never had all the gadgets you have now, you know, your iPods and all that. We had one good old station, KTKT, and they played all of John's and my favorite songs.

Now, it is hard for me to admit this, even today, after all these years. But, you see, Mamma knew I was pregnant and she was, you know, a lady through and through and getting pregnant at seventeen was not something privileged young ladies did. She actually had guessed I was pregnant, which shocked me because I thought I was hiding it well. It was a rough evening and she was so calm that she rattled my nerves. "Young lady, you need to go to your room until your daddy gets home. Is this what we taught you? I just cannot imagine what your father will say if he does not kill you first. Why did you not wait until your wedding night? Emily, I just don't understand you. How could you do this to us? What will people say? And John, is he the …," she stopped mid-sentence and I remember she could not bring herself to ask me if John was the father. You have to understand, Mamma was the kind of person who would get upset when I wore different earrings in each ear. This was too much for her to take. She was from Texas, a real lady.

"Yes, Mamma, he is," I remember telling her, "and he loves me." The calm exterior she had been showing vanished as soon as I said those words and she stood up, straightened her red silk caftan and put her freshly manicured hands on her petite hips. "Go to your room now." I did.

Now, don't go telling your mother that I am sharing this story with you, but as soon as Mamma shut the door to my room, I got my clothes, and twenty dollars that I had saved up working at the movies and snuck out the window to meet John. I guess we sort of knew in our hearts that this would happen once the parents got involved. What did they know about love anyway?

John, oh my John, he looked so handsome that day. With his red hair and baby brown eyes. He was a whole foot taller than me and I tell you, spent half his life in those same jeans and white sneakers. He was the son of the only dentist in our town and I tell you, like the cobbler's kids with no shoes, he had the worst teeth! I think he smoked too much. But I loved him. We met in school when we were both in third grade and there was no separating us, you know? People would laugh at first and call us the real "Odd Couple" but even the teachers knew we shared a special bond.

I stopped my story to sip my tea and to savor the looks on the anticipatory faces of my audience. They were so precious. Hard to believe I was that young once. Everything hurt, everything was loose, and everything sagged. I guess being sixty-five will do that to you.

"Go on," one of them pleaded.

Where was I? Ah, we were in the car. The Odd Couple, headed to Vegas. We had a little money, enough for a few days and then, well, you know, we did not think of then. We thought of now. Love would carry us, we thought, we hoped and we believed.

John had packed smartly and we had water, beer, and two boxes of Big Hunks, candy cigarettes, licorice pipes, and my all-time favorite, Sugar Daddy pops. The roads were empty as we drove through the early morning hours and finally reached Motel 9 at the border of Arizona and Nevada, at around 3:00 am.

The rooms were expensive, I remember. Six dollars a night. But the room was cool and had a clean bed and running water! We left all our stuff there and then John and I got in the car and drove to the Serenity Chapel about two miles west. It was one of those twenty-four-hour wedding places, you know. And yes, in a matter of minutes, no questions asked (for an extra two dollars), we were husband and wife by three-forty-five! I will never forget the time, the chapel was so crowded, you would have thought it was five in the evening. A few people even toasted our union. My only regret is that we were in jeans, I always wanted to have a white dress and all that! A kind woman lent me her veil and another one lent me some flowers. We had no rings, so John and I just placed kisses on each other's hands. Who needed symbols of love when we had each other?

We had done it. I was so happy, I think I was the happiest I have ever been in my life on that day. I had everything I ever wanted. As he kissed me, and held my hand, and promised to make it all okay, I knew that God had forgiven me for getting pregnant before tying the knot. But, all that was ancient history. We were married and now ready to live a life together and have a baby.

As we drove towards the motel, John noticed that there were police cars everywhere. Daddy had found us. I should have known. My father was the mayor and as you can imagine he knew everyone. He reversed and we began to take the road toward Sedona.

They would never find us and besides, we had to celebrate. John had hidden a bottle of wine under the seat and we opened it. "To my Emily, I will love you forever and ever, if you ever lose me, just call me, I will always be there," the wind carried his words and we laughed and toasted in tiny paper cups. The road began to fly by. We opened a few beers and began to celebrate, the music blaring, I lay down with my head on his lap and closed my eyes. Thank you, God.

I stopped my story.

I needed more tea and now, I was not sure if they were yet ready to hear the rest.

I had to tell them.

Jena, Lisa, that was the last time I ever saw your grandfather. He lost control of the car on a turn and we were hit by an oncoming car. I woke up in the hospital with my father standing next to my bed. John, ah .... John, he, well, he

.... he did not make it. Your mamma ... she ... she did, safe in my womb, she made it, along with me.

He is still here, you know, I can feel him. I can hear him. I see him in your faces, in your eyes, and even your hair. Red, just like Grandpa John.

Glossary

Amchi Mumbai – Our Mumbai

Arre; Arre baba – slang for hey. Baba, here, is person

Bai – Lady

Beedi - inexpensive smoke

Beta – Child (mostly for a boy but also used affectionately for a girl)

Bhagwan - God

Chalo, chalo Let's go, Let's go

Chikna - Fair skinned good looking man

Chowki – a small stool

Dadi – Paternal grandmother

Desiland - India

Devadasis – Dancers of the temples

Di – Short for didi meaning sister.

Diae - midwife

Didi - Sister

Dosa – A crepe like dish prepared with lentils and rice

Dupatta - a scarf

Halwa – a dessert

Hanuman Mandir – Temple dedicated to Lord Hanuman, The Monkey God

Hijra; guru hijra – These are transsexuals. Guru is the teacher or the leader of a group

Kuccha homes – these are temporary homes

Kurta pajama – An Indian outfit – loose pants and a long shirt

Majhi – boatman

Mangalsutra – a customary beaded necklace worn by married women

Mousambi - orange juice

Na - no

O-kaeri nasai – welcome home

Okasaan _ mother

Paan – beter leaf

Piyo - drink

Raakhi – a ceremonial thread tied by a sister on her brother's wrist.

Salwaar kameez – A traditional Indian outfit – loose pants and a long shirt.

Sindoor – a vermillion powder that married women wear in their hair parting to show that they are married.

Thali -plate

Thullas - cops

Yaar - friend

ACKNOWLEDGEMENTS

This book is dedicated to Cheryl Tan. You are reading it because Cheryl Tan believed in me and chose one of my stories for inclusion in her lovely book, Singapore Noir.

Thanks to my husband, Sameer, my sweet boys, my parents, my sister, my brother-in-law, my very supportive sister-in-law and her husband, my adoring mother-in-law and my biggest supporter – my late father-in-law, and the rest of my sweet family for standing by me as I worked on this for what seems like a lifetime.

I stand by my feeling that it takes a village to write a book. So I want to thank my village:

My amazing supportive FB team and beta readers- Judy Kreloff, Wendy Read, Elizabeth Young, Mollie Cox Bryan, Chris Walker, Meghana Bhave, Vrinda Deval, Reetika Gupta Kohli, Ana Di, Judy Witts Francini, Andrea Lynn, Daphne Howland, Betty Ann Besa-Quirino, Aviva Goldfarb, Stan Santos, Alka Keswani, Prachee Deshpande, Kalyani, Luca Marchiori, Charmian Christie, Ramin Ganeshram, Janis Mclean, Alison Singh Gee, Kara Newman, Andrea Meyers, Sydny Miner, Suzanne Rafer, Fred Minnick, Sandra Beckwith, Bethanne Patrick, Andrea McCarthy, Nisha Sidhu, Monica Sethi, Ali Guleria, Sean Gardner, Nevin martin, Jessica Strelitz, Amy Rea and all those whom I have forgotten to add here.

To my sweet friends who stood by me as I cancelled lunches and dinners in order to "just finish the book already" – Donna Berk, Debbie Tosi, Kathy Alsegaf, Kat Flinn, Mike Klozar, Marcia Tomson, Ana Borray, Britt Jackman, Susan Koch, Rosalba Acosta, Eman Safadi, Rami Safadi, Katie Farquhar, Sandy Turba and Ya-Roo Yang.

The superb cover for this book was designed by James at Humblenations.com. He is terrific and I highly recommend his work. I could not have asked for a better editor than Suzanne Fass. THANK YOU.

ABOUT THE AUTHOR

I am an engineer turned food writer based out of Washington, D.C.. I have been published in many major national and international publications, including *Food & Wine*, *The New York Times*, *Parents*, *Cooking Light*, *Prevention*, *AARP-The magazine*, *Health*, *SELF*, *Bon Appetit*, *Saveur*, and many more. My food essays have been included in Best Food Writing anthologies (2005, 2009, 2010, 2014). I have published three cookbooks, the latest being: Modern Spice: Inspired Indian recipes for the contemporary Kitchen (Simon & Schuster, 2009. In 2012, The Chicago Tribune picked me as one of seven note-worthy food writers to watch.

I am a frequent speaker at the Smithsonian, NPR and many other prestigious outlets.

My first fiction short story - MOTHER - has been published by Akashic Books in their collection Singapore Noir that released on June 7th 2014

You can contact me via my website: monicabhide.com